A PART OF VIRTUE

Murder seemed grimly out of place amid the Cotswolds, but Chuck Lindop was undoubtedly dead at the caravan site he ran as manager, and Inspector Crow was there to find out why. There had been a lot of comings and goings at the site, and many of those involved had a grudge against Chuck. There had also been a spate of burglaries in which Chuck might have been involved, and someone – possibly Chuck – had been conspiring with the thieving gipsies, in town for the annual fair. A complex case with some challenging problems, which Crow solved in his own inimitable way.

A PART OF VIRTUE

A PART OF VIRTUE

by

Roy Lewis

Dales Large Print Books
Long Preston, North Yorkshire,
BD23 4ND, England.

British Library Cataloguing in Publication Data.

Lewis, Roy
    A part of virtue.

    A catalogue record of this book is
    available from the British Library

    ISBN   978-1-84262-675-7 pbk

First published in Great Britain in 1975
by William Collins Sons & Co. Ltd.

Copyright © Roy Lewis 1975

Cover illustration © Dave Wall by arrangement with
Arcangel Images

The moral right of the author has been asserted

Published in Large Print 2009 by arrangement with
Mr Roy Lewis

Dales Large Print is an imprint of Library Magna Books Ltd.

Printed and bound in Great Britain by
T.J. (International) Ltd., Cornwall, PL28 8RW

CHAPTER I

1

Andrew found the cheap, black-and-gold tin trinket box in the corner of the suitcase pushed under the bed. If there had been a key to it, it had been lost years ago. A Christmas present from his mother, the box had been intended to serve as a money-box, but he had always used it for his personal possessions – those possessions that held secret memories for him.

He hadn't changed over the years.

The box contained a thin pile of photographs, half a dozen cuttings from newspapers, a piece of faded silk – he had no idea where *that* came from – and a ticket to a concert in the Albert Hall. He picked up one of the cuttings and read it.

'On Saturday, at St Giles's Church, Andrew Keene to Sara, only daughter of John and Phyllis Rowland.'

He remembered the contrast between the greyness of the massive stone church with its hundred-feet tower, and the intense blue of the Saturday morning sky, washed clean by an overnight storm for his ten o'clock marriage. He could recall walking from the hired car and staring at the battlemented and pinnacled nave roof, wondering how it was he had never really *looked* at the church before. Then there had been the stained glass explosion of colour inside, a sharp dagger of light picking at his father-in-law's thinning hair, exposing the pale scalp, and glinting on the red rims of his mother-in-law's spectacles. Dead now, both of them, within a year of the marriage of their only daughter to Andrew Keene. A car crash, after visiting Andrew and Sara, still quarrelling, probably, such a *final* way of expressing disapproval of a marriage they had thought should never have taken place.

It had left Sara without the buttress of her mother and father; Andrew was the only person to rely on, to lean on when she wanted to lean.

He picked up the pile of photographs and there he was, thin and insubstantial as a sapling, dark-suited, pale-faced, squinting anxiously into the camera and clutching Sara's hand as the small wedding group clustered behind. Sara looked magnificent, as always. Tall, almost as tall as he was; a confident smile on her face – a handsome face rather than a beautiful one – and the tiny hint of panic in her eyes. It was the sun, she used to say, but it wasn't, Andrew knew it wasn't, because he knew about the uncertainties wriggling around beneath the display of strength and confidence. They made a fine pair, people had said, both young and eager and happy, such a well-matched pair. But they said it with the urgency of disbelief, papering over the cracks of their surprise when they saw Andrew's shyness and diffidence and lack of *colour*.

Behind their hands they would whisper, 'What on earth does Sara see in him?'

Andrew put down the box and looked through the rest of the photographs. There was the shot of the lurid sunset he had taken from the window of the van – it had been the first week they had been here, when they had been excited as children, at their new, compact home, their first home. Then there was the view from the farm down the lane, looking up across the field where they saw the hares in the early dawns and late evenings – the dark line of the trees hiding the main road, the cream caravans lined up martially beyond the hedge as though daring the complacent cattle to intrude. Carefully, Andrew counted the vans in the photograph. Thirty, most of them unoccupied, as he remembered. Their caravan was just to the left of centre in the photograph, near the trees. There were only about twenty vans on the site now, eight of them not lived in.

The park had never really been a financial proposition, he was sure of that. Not enough people, not enough money coming in. He and Sara, they had thought it would be different – maybe that was the trouble really. They had seen the new site in a glowing haze two years ago – their first home, they would make it a loving home, and they'd watch as others came to the site, children arrived, a clubhouse was built, a swimming-pool ... a *community*.

If it had happened, maybe things would have been different. Somehow, with only twenty vans on the site the gaping vacant areas were depressing, and if the rabbits did come capering through the grass at night, eyes glinting in the flashlights, it was little compensation.

He heard a step behind him.

'For Christ's *sake,* Andrew, what are you *doing?*'

Sheepishly, Andrew put down the box, rose to his feet and followed Sara out of the bedroom into the living area of the van. Mr Forsyth was sitting in the far corner with his left shoulder leaning against the window, the cup of coffee Sara had made him half-finished on the collapsible table in front of him. He was about fifty years of age, dressed in a respectable bookmaker's suit, discreet check, blue shirt, stained tie, white handkerchief in his top pocket. The strips of bushy hair that made him look like a tonsured monk were matched by thick furred brows that were just now ridged into a frown of discontent. Stubby fingers drummed unhappily on the table; his red-veined nose twitched vaguely as though sniffing for suspects; his whole appearance was one of faded belligerence. He would like to be angrier but as yet he had no grounds; he would like to be stern, but he lacked the energy; he knew right was on his side but could not yet prove it, and meanwhile he was unhappy, and nervous, and upset, and disinclined to drink any more coffee.

Andrew stood above him, leaning forward slightly, always afraid his head would touch the roof of the van, though it never did.

'I'm sorry, Mr Forsyth, I don't seem to be able to put my hands on it right now.'

'You looked everywhere?' Forsyth asked in a regimental bark.

'Everywhere I can think of.' Andrew looked towards Sara, seeking support, but she was staring fixedly at Forsyth, her arms folded, resting over the bulge of her stomach, her mouth expressing discontent matching that of Forsyth, her eyes holding that old hint of anxiety he knew so well. 'I'm sure it'll turn up,' Andrew added lamely.

The stubby fingers changed to a marching air, the drums of an advancing troop. The bushy eyebrows grew closer together as though seeking moral support.

11

'You appreciate my position,' he announced gruffly, a statement not a question.

'Naturally,' Andrew murmured.

'I mean, if you haven't got it, what proof is there?'

'I'm sure it will turn up, Mr Forsyth.'

'Yes, but in the meanwhile, what's to be done? You sure you've looked everywhere?'

Andrew gestured vaguely towards the small bedroom. 'If it's anywhere, it'll be in there. I mean, there's not many places to look in a van, Mr Forsyth.'

'Quite. Quite so. But it leaves me in a difficult situation, you'll understand that.' He drummed away again, impatiently. 'Two years, you say?'

'That's right,' Andrew said. 'We got married at Easter and then we moved into the van here almost right away. You know, we had a brief honeymoon, and then came down to look at these vans. We liked the site – the trees, and the view across to the hills, we were taken by it, you know – so we put down a deposit straight away because we understood Easter would be a time when lots of people would be thinking of buying vans, before the summer, you know–'

'Humph.'

Andrew paused, but Forsyth added nothing to his comment, so he went on. 'Then, about a month after we'd moved in, the question of a hiring and later purchase was no longer necessary, because, well, Sarah got some money and we were able to buy the van outright.'

'I gave the money to you,' Sara said almost accusingly.

'And I bought the van,' Andrew said. Their eyes met for a moment, as they both thought of Mr and Mrs Rowland, excited and angry here at the van that last night, then driving homeward to a collision with a lorry and death. There had been so little money, enough to buy the van outright, £800, and then about two thousand pounds as a building society investment they didn't want to touch until the baby came.

'But there's no receipt,' Forsyth said.

'There *was* a receipt, I'm sure of it,' Andrew replied.

'But you can't find it.'

Andrew opened his mouth but there seemed to be nothing to say so he closed it again. He stood there feeling vaguely foolish, not knowing what to do, what to say. He would have offered Forsyth another cup of coffee but he hadn't finished the one in front of him. Forsyth heaved a deep, disappointed sigh.

'I don't understand it.' He peered out of the window towards the vans on the slope below. 'This has never gone the way it should have. An investment this was, for me. I gave up the farm down there, kept this

13

field as an investment, good open site, chance to make a regular income, but you know, it's been hopeless. Oh, I tied the ends up all right–'

'I'm sure you did, Mr Forsyth.'

'Tied them up by putting in lights, concreting the sites, getting a site manager, advertising, but somehow the people never came. Dammit, what's happening to the holiday industry? You'd think here in the Cotswolds there'd be people enough to want to stay overnight, week-ends, couple of weeks maybe. All right, I only took out twenty licences for permanent residents because I wanted the overnight trade, but as it's gone on I've got neither. Not enough permanents, not enough overnighters, not enough week-enders. I wish I'd never started the damn thing.'

Forsyth looked around the van as though blaming it for his own troubles. 'And you've got no receipt to show me,' he said mournfully. 'You understand my position?'

Andrew made a vague gesture that could be interpreted as assent or dissent, whichever struck the right chord for Forsyth. Sara glared at him, her dark eyes suddenly snapping with an anger that had overridden her uncertainties.

'No, *I* don't understand your position, Mr Forsyth. I know *our* position. We own this van. We paid good money for it.'

'But the receipt—'

'Andrew signed several papers,' she interrupted. 'If we can't put our hands on the receipt for the moment that's one thing, but I don't see how it affects you in any way at all really. I mean, you haven't told us *why* you want to see the receipt anyway.'

'Proof of ownership, I suppose,' Andrew said. Sara's eyes snapped at him, warning him to stay quiet now she was launched, and whose side was he on anyway?

'We bought this van for eight hundred pounds,' Sara said stubbornly. 'The receipt will turn up, believe me, if I have to take the place apart. But I don't see why I have to. Why can't you just ask Chuck Lindop?'

Forsyth's eyes were small and red-rimmed. They half closed now, as though wanting to shut out the realities of the world. He pursed his lips, sucked in his breath thoughtfully, until there was a light whistling sound between his teeth.

'My site manager doesn't seem to be on the site today. Nor was he here last week when I called. In fact, he always seems to be otherwise engaged when I try to contact him.'

'There's the phone, Mr Forsyth,' Sara said, almost rudely.

'When it works,' Forsyth replied non-committally.

'Well, I think you'll just have to ask Mr

Lindop,' Sara insisted. 'It's not for us to produce a receipt. We've been living here for two years now, and it's obvious we own the van. We don't pay hire-purchase, do we? All we pay is the usual ground rent, once a year, and a few charges that Chuck Lindop put up at the park entrance, and I don't agree with those either, but as far as a receipt is concerned why don't you just ask Lindop? It was he who sold the van to us, anyway. It'll be there in his books, and he's supposed to be site manager, even if he isn't here half the time, so I think it's him you ought to chase up, not me and Andrew.'

Forsyth thought it over briefly. His little eyes flickered around the van, almost possessively, and then he shrugged. 'I suppose so. But I'd be grateful if you *could* look out that receipt. I'll get out of your way now, anyway, and wait up at the office for a while. I suppose my manager *will* condescend to return soon.'

The coffee cup almost went over as he struggled to rise from behind the table. He righted it, nodded a short goodbye and stepped out of the van. Andrew stood in the doorway and looked down at him.

'I'll look for it again, Mr Forsyth.'

Forsyth nodded grumpily and walked across the grass towards where his Rover was parked on the flinty roadway that had been laid through the site but never completed

16

with tarmac. He stared moodily at his tyres before getting into his car. He drove the sixty yards to the green-and-cream van that served the site manager as an office, then killed the engine, lit a pipe and sat silently in the car. Andrew turned back into the van. Sara was still standing against the partition that screened the gas cooker and the tiny sink from the living area.

'I could do with a coffee,' Andrew said.

She made no reply. She was staring fixedly at the thinly carpeted floor as though she had never seen it before; there was a fierce intensity in her gaze that told him trouble was boiling up again. He filled the kettle, lit the gas, boiled the water and made two cups of instant coffee. He set them down on the table.

'Sara—'

'You make me sick!'

Andrew sat down. He gestured vaguely towards the table.

'Your coffee—'

'Stuff the coffee! What the hell's the matter with you, Andrew? Why didn't you tell that man Forsyth what to do with his bloody receipt? Just because he owns the site, it doesn't mean he can come poking his nose here, into our van, demanding this and that—'

'He didn't demand—'

'What does he want the thing for anyway?

17

I suppose you did *get* a receipt from Chuck Lindop! I wouldn't put it past you if you didn't. Why the hell I didn't see to that myself at the time I can't imagine, but I suppose in love's young dream I was still in the position where I thought it was the husband who did things! I've learned a bloody sight different since, I can tell you. I mean, did he give you a receipt?'

'I'm pretty sure–'

'Pretty sure!' she mocked him. 'For God's sake, Andrew, do you have to be so stupid? And when you were there in the bedroom looking for it – this non-existent receipt – what the hell were you up to? On your knees looking at bloody photographs! You know, I despair, I really do. I guess that's how you were at work, that's really why you got the push, they found an excuse and got rid of you not because you were redundant but because you simply day-dreamed all the day. When are you going to pull yourself together? When are you going to recognize your responsibilities? Not only to me – damn it, pretty soon there are other responsibilities with the baby coming, and I just can't cope if I'm going to be messed about with worries, like this man Forsyth coming in here and unsettling things worse than they are–'

There was a light thump just inside the door. Andrew looked up and there was the mongrel, Patch, grinning at him. Andrew managed a grin back and as though by way of salute Patch lifted a leg and urinated against the cooker.

2

'You *naughty* beast!'

Ruby Sanders came in through the doorway like an overdressed tornado, grabbed up the happy dog and pitched him out through the door. Almost in the same movement she turned, reached for a cloth and a plastic bowl and ran the tap as she announced, 'Don't worry, love, I'll see to it. My dog, my problem, it's just that he likes Andrew, gets excited when he sees him and away he goes. Don't fret, I'll wipe it up, over in a jiffy.'

'That's the washing-up bowl,' Sara wailed in helpless fury. 'And the cloth!'

'Need a new one anyway. Drop one in this afternoon. Got some on offer in the super-market at Stowford yesterday.'

She was crouching beside the cooker, bowl of water on the floor, mopping up Patch's contribution, seemingly unaware of Sarah's furious silence. She was a short, compact woman with china blue eyes that held an innocence at strong variance with her language, experience and inclinations. Her mouth was wide, usually open, often talking, and generous in its offerings. Her hair was always elaborately coiffured and firmly subjugated by lashings of lacquer and her clothes were just a centimetre too tight or too short or too revealing. She had a predilection for frills which were unbecoming; today she was wearing pale blue trousers that clung to her thighs, hips and bottom in a desperate attempt to retain a fibrous contact under the threat of splitting, and her blouse was ruffled absurdly at throat, bosom and wrist – an odd amalgam of party best and working impracticality. She rose, her slacks sighing and rustling with relief, squeezed out the cloth, deposited it in the waste bin, threw the water out of the doorway, washed her hands and smiled brightly.

'I'd love a cup of coffee,' she said, and made one for herself.

She was thirty and, in her own words, had known 'more than a few fellers'.

'So tell me what's on, then,' Ruby said and sipped enthusiastically at her coffee.

'What do you mean?' Sara asked. She was sitting down now, grudgingly drinking the coffee Andrew had made for her, and with an equal reluctance accepting Ruby's thick-skinned presence in her van. Atmosphere was something Ruby never noticed, Andrew guessed: she could come into the middle of a quarrel, or enter the van when a young married couple had decided it was bedtime, and she could sit and talk, impervious as rubber, round, soft, persistent, and completely and utterly self-centred. She chuckled now, and Andrew liked her for her chuckle, her common giggle, her uncomplicated personality.

'Forsyth,' she said.

'What about him?' Sara asked, giving nothing away.

'Oh, come *on*,' Ruby insisted. 'You know as well as I do old Jack Forsyth don't come around here unless there's trouble brewing. As far as this site is concerned he's an absentee landlord. You got to remember, I been here on this site four years now, before you – and for that matter before Chuck Lindop – got here. And in that time I seen Jack Forsyth here maybe four times. First time was when the council raised hell over the mains, second time was when the gipsies heading for Stowford Fair tried to camp here on the site and he came over with the coppers from Netherfield. The others I don't recall too well but they was trouble times, so this must be one too.'

'I don't know what you're talking about,' Sara said coldly.

She found Ruby difficult to handle, Andrew guessed. Sara had changed over this last year. When he met her first she had been a little shy, but her personality was warm, and she had an enthusiasm for personal relationships of a close kind that made her very lovable. She was a dependent person, one who *wanted* to be looked after, and he supposed it was in this way that he had failed her. He knew as well as anyone that he was not to be depended upon; he was a weak reed; he needed support as much as she did for he lacked the necessary steel to deal with people and situations when they turned ugly. Ruby Sanders wasn't like that. She had a streak of coarseness that enabled her to face the harsher aspects of life, a capacity to overcome vicissitudes that he envied and Sara could not understand. Ruby was difficult to keep out of your caravan; her own warmth spilled over into cunning and Sara could never tell where the one started and the other ended. It could be friendliness or calculation; open-handedness or manipulation; but whatever it was it was *confusing*, and Sara could not handle her. She liked people to be straight and uncomplicated. Men should be male and strong and reliable. Women should be pliant – as she wanted to be pliant, and was not. But Ruby fitted no pattern. She was a woman who had found her own way of life in a male world; she had been used often enough, but she did her own share of using, too.

'Well, it's something to do with Chuck Lindop, that's obvious,' Ruby said.

'Why do you suggest that?' Sara asked.

'Like I said, love, it's obvious. Look here, Jack Forsyth isn't the kind of chap who socializes. If he's come here on to the site, on to his *investment*, it's because something's up. I been watching him. He arrived about three, didn't he? He parked outside Chuck's van there, went in for a chat with the Sharkeys on Site Nine. By three-thirty he was over with the Wilsons. Four o'clock he was with you. And stayed best part of an hour. Count up the way I do and the chances are he got what he was after here – specially since he's now up the field sitting outside Chuck's van, waiting for Chuck to come back from wherever he is. But I'll bet you a pound to a penny Chuck don't come back while old Forsyth is here. Got antennae, Chuck has; antennae that tell him there's trouble waiting. And he don't turn up unless it's the kind of trouble he wants.' She scratched her cheek wonderingly. 'Thing is, what did Forsyth want from you two nice young people?'

Andrew glanced uncertainly towards Sara, who glared at him to maintain silence.

'I think Mr Forsyth is of the opinion that the site manager doesn't spend enough time on the site,' she said.

Ruby grinned. 'That's true enough, for

sure. There've been times when he rarely left, of course.' Something happened to her china blue eyes, a dark hint of regret and pain, but it was gone in a moment and replaced by a calculated malice. 'And not so long ago either, once I'd moved down the field – or *been* moved, I should say.' Her grin came again, broadened into a chuckle as some private joke touched her. 'Fact is, that man's got so many irons in the fire he don't have *time* to stay on the site.'

'Presumably Mr Forsyth pays him an adequate wage to look after it.'

'Presumably,' Ruby mimicked, not un-kindly. 'Yes, he does in fact, pays him a reasonable screw, but Chuck never did see this site managership as a job for life. Am-bitious, he is. I could tell you things...'

She lapsed into a sudden silence. Andrew watched her as she placed both hands around her coffee cup and stared at the coffee. She was a moody person; her general devil-may-care gaiety made her attractive to men, good company, easy to get on with, but there were occasions when life suddenly got through to her again and she was touched by dark thoughts, realizations of pain when the self-induced drug of extroversion wore off and she felt exposed and raw and vulnerable. It was happening briefly now, and he was aware of the coarseness of her skin, the enlarged pores at the base of her rather large nose, the liberal make-up around her mouth and eyes.

Maybe that was how Sara always saw her. Andrew looked at his wife and observed how Sara had lost the critical downturn to her mouth as she noticed Ruby's sudden vulnerability. She stood up, awkwardly, manœuvring away from the table with difficulty, one hand on her spreading belly.

'Another coffee, Ruby?'

'Hell, no, haven't finished this one. And you sit down, can't have you trundling around with that little one kicking inside you. How long is it now, by the way?'

Sara shrugged. 'Five weeks, they say. I feel like a mountain. Makes me short-tempered.'

It was the nearest she could get to an apology for her shortness and Ruby knew it. She waved a deprecating hand.

'Ain't we all short-tempered? Anyway, talk of that Chuck Lindop always makes me a bit mad, you know. I mean, when he moved me from where I was down closer to the lavatories I was so hopping I could have stuck a breadknife into him. Almost did, as a matter of fact, you know that?' The grin was back. 'You know what the bastard did? Chucked me a loaf. What can you do with a guy like that? You wave a knife at him and he makes you laugh! I mean, if it had been a proper loaf – but *sliced* bread!'

A light thump told them that Patch had

returned with a leap into the van. Sara glowered but Ruby seemed not to notice. She put out her hand and Patch swaggered forward, confident in being loved. He licked her fingers.

'Didn't like you, did he, Patch? Put the boot up your backside a few times. Said dogs fouled up the camp site, and you do too, don't you? I usually get him to go up against Lindop's van, you know that? When it's dark. Well, you got to take every chance you can get to manage your own back. But you stay away from him, Patch, you hear me? Stay well away.'

Patch dropped his rump, stretched out and muzzled his paws. Sara said, 'He won't be able to come in here, Ruby, not when the baby comes.'

'He likes kids!'

'It'll be unhygienic!'

'Not that we'll be here long, anyway,' Sara announced.

Ruby looked from her to Andrew in surprise.

'You leaving after the baby comes? Is that why Forsyth was around here then? You didn't tell me you were going!'

Andrew shook his head. 'It's not something we've really discussed ourselves yet. Of course, we don't want to stay here longer than we have to – I mean, a caravan site is no place to bring up a baby, even if it is fairly close to the quarry for me. But we've not decided anything yet.'

'We'll be moving,' Sara said firmly.

'If we can afford it,' Andrew said.

'We've *got* to afford it, even if it means moving back to Oxford. If you'd only kept that bloody job of yours instead of getting made redundant things would have been better. We could have had some prospect to look forward to. Now, in that bloody quarry...'

'Oh, oh,' Ruby said. 'Marital fall-out. Thank God I never walked to the altar. There was a chap once, but we discovered I wasn't pregnant after all so he scarpered pretty quick after that... So you'll be selling the van, then?'

If we can prove it's ours, Andrew thought, but said nothing as he caught the warning glint in Sara's eye. 'We'll be selling,' she said firmly.

Ruby shook her head. 'Won't be easy, you know. Chuck, he's got a bloody good racket going, you know that? For starters, he sells the van on commission from Jack Forsyth. So he gets a rake-off for every van he sells. Every site gets filled, he gets a percentage on that. But when you want to sell yourself, he gets the right to veto the sale – you can't just sell to anyone on this site. He has to approve it. And that means you pay a fee for the approval – or you don't get it.'

'We can sell off the site,' Sara said indignantly.

'Sure, but you have to pay him a fee before you can get the bloody van off!'

'He can't stop us moving it!'

'Watch him do it! How you going to get a lorry on to the site to pull your van off if he refuses a lorry driver permission to come on to the site? You want to read the small print in your site contract, love. I tell you Chuck Lindop, and through him Jack Forsyth I suppose, has got us by the short and curlies every time.'

'Is this right, Andrew?' Sara asked. Her face had plumped out since the beginning of her pregnancy and she looked fine and healthy, but she had developed a tendency towards reddening at the slightest provocation. She was getting flushed now.

'Well, I suppose so, I don't really know. I haven't read our contract for some time, but it may be there in the small print. I understand there are certain controls over van sales on the site; the idea is to make sure that undesirable persons don't move on without permission. I mean, a sale could be made to a family that was … unsuitable, or something.'

Ruby was laughing at him openly, her red lips wide, her gums exposed above her white teeth. *'Unsuitable,'* she gurgled happily. 'That's a laugh. The only way someone could be unsuitable to Chuck Lindop would be if he had no money. But you take my word for it, lovers, you won't find it easy to sell off this site. And make your profit, that is.'

Sara leaned forward suspiciously. 'How do you mean, make your profit?'

'Oh, come on, kid. You know in the main these residential vans hold their price. You pay six hundred pounds for one, couple of years you should be still able to get about five hundred pounds or more for it, because the newer models would have gone up maybe two hundred quid. But that's the come-on that you're given by an operator like Chuck Lindop. The realities are different.'

'Tell me,' Sara said grimly.

'Simple enough,' Ruby said, obviously enjoying the opportunity to air her knowledge of the world to these young unsophisticates. 'You decide to sell your van, right? You tell Chuck, because after all it's in your site agreement that he has first offer, so the van can stay on the site for letting purposes. I mean, it *is* all but bedded in, isn't it, with running water and everything? Okay. So you go to him, you tell him, he gives you that great, warm, wide smile of his and he says of course he'll make you an offer. What about three hundred pounds for the van you paid twice that much for?'

Ruby settled back in her chair; Patch raised his head briefly, calculated Ruby wasn't about to leave and settled down again.

'I'd tell him what he could do with his three hundred pounds,' Sara said.

'So you'd tell him. Who wouldn't? Pete Orton did. But he sold out to Chuck eventually. And at a lower price, too.'

'But why?'

'Because it was costing him not to!' Ruby shook her head. 'Peter had retired, took the van for a year, decided he didn't really like the air after all and wanted to return to Oxford. Chuck made him a poor offer for his van and Pete told him what he could do with his money. Like you're going to, hey? Well, come winter that van was still here, Pete was still paying rent for it, travelling up from Oxford week-ends to show people over it, and what happened? Nobody prepared to buy. Why not? Because every time Pete found a buyer Chuck queered the whole thing. Either he wouldn't allow a truck on the site, or he didn't approve of the buyers, or he wasn't prepared to allow them in unless they paid him a commission – it was hell for the old man. So he took the easy way in the end. He gave in. Sold to Chuck. Following week the van was moved off the site and that was that. But you tell me things will be different with you? Maybe. But let me see it.' She gestured towards Sara's hands lightly resting on her stomach. 'With Pete Orton it was retirement and shortage of cash. With you ... will you hold out for long with a baby around?'

'Chuck Lindop may be inclined to be more helpful towards us,' Sara said.

Ruby gave her a calculating look. 'He's always more helpful towards women – if there's no man around. But then it's just that the payment's different. But like I said, things may be different with you. I'm just giving you kids a warning. Don't expect generosity from our site manager – it's a condition too close to miraculous to be expected... Who's up there with Forsyth?'

Sara twisted slightly in her seat so that she could look out past the curtains to the top of the site. Andrew stooped also to peer out. The flint track curved slightly along the sixty yards to Chuck Lindop's van, which also served as a site office. Flanking the track, some thirty feet away on each side, were the unoccupied vans, and parked near the top one was Jack Forsyth's Rover. Beside it was a burly man with matted, curly hair and a leather jacket and jeans.

'It's Mr Samson,' Sara said.

'He's talking with Forsyth?' Ruby rose, peered out of the window. She had lost some of her confidence; her eyes were brighter and she seemed a little breathless. In another person it could have been nervousness, but in Ruby it could have had different roots and causes. She leaned over Sara to peer out;

31

Sara smiled at her. There was an edge of malice in her voice when she said, 'Pity you're so far down the site, Ruby, isn't it?'

For just a second anger scored Ruby's face. She looked down at Sara as though about to make a sharp retort but she glanced swiftly at Andrew and bit it back. Her mouth relaxed. She managed a grin. 'A walk down the site never does any man harm, Sara. But I'd better get along.'

Sara wouldn't let it go. In the old days, before they were married, and when they were newly married, she would never have let rancour touch her eyes or her words.

'Yes, you'd better hurry, Ruby. I gather he likes to have his slippers warmed for him.'

She was tangling with the wrong person. Ruby produced her falsest smile. 'There are some women who keep *nothing* warm for their men,' she said, and called to Patch to follow her. With an apologetic look towards Andrew, Patch followed.

3

'That was uncalled for.'

'You started it, Sara.'

'Why is it you never stick up for me, but always take the other person's point of view?'

It was an argument that was now almost

exhausted. In the forty minutes that had passed since Ruby Sanders had left their van Andrew and Sara had gone over the same bickering ground. When Sara accused Andrew of taking sides with Ruby against his wife he disagreed. Sara accused Andrew of liking Ruby and he agreed – he did. She was open, honest – relatively honest, anyway – and uncomplicated. She was also a whore, Sara announced. Andrew stepped back from that one.

But there were signs of Sara's winding down. She felt tired. The baby had been active today, Forsyth's visit had unsettled her, and she was feeling generally out of sorts and dissatisfied with herself. Andrew understood how she felt; she was too aware of her condition, too concerned about her appearance. Where some women held their pregnancy proudly Sara did not. They had not intended making a baby. Now, the baby was coming. Sara resented it. Andrew kept away from that one too.

But, inevitably, after supper when Sara was rested the arguments started again. What had Forsyth been hinting at? Was the sale of the van to Andrew and Sara legal? Had Andrew ever received a bill of sale from Chuck Lindop? It went on and on, the words grinding at him, and he tried to read in the gaslight as the summer evening closed in. His head began to ache. He heard cars leaving the site and Sara moved on to a new tack.

Here she was, twenty-two years old, and already she was house-bound. No, not even house-bound. Van-bound! Everyone was going out tonight, heading for Stowford and the fair. What had she seen of it? Nothing! There had been a time when they used to go out nights, but not now. And there was Ruby going off again. She supposed *she'd* have a good time and she was nearly ten years older than Andrew Keene's wife! It was all so unfair.

'Be sensible Sara,' Andrew said irritably. 'You can't go out to Stowford on the bus the way you're feeling.'

'We could go if you had a car.'

'Well, I haven't got a car!'

'You'd have a car if you had a better job!'

Andrew grimaced angrily. 'We'd have a car if you drew that money out of the building society too, but that's not the point. The money stays there because we'll need it, when the baby's growing, and when we can afford a mortgage to buy a house. But in the meanwhile, there's no car, we live in a van, I've got a job at the quarry and it's the best I can do for the moment.'

'It's about the best you'll ever be able to do!' she flashed.

'The marriage service says for better or worse.'

'And worse it is!'

'As you like, Sara. But keep your voice down. And let's drop this futile argument.'

'It's all very well for you. You get off the site during the day. You haven't been stuck here the way I've been stuck here for two years, hardly anyone to talk to. And you can get out nights–'

'I never do!'

'But you *can,* if you want to, and I *can't!* I'm stuck here, fat, pregnant–'

Words rose inside him like worms, harsh words with knife edges, words that could peel back skin and expose nerve ends, rip open old wounds and create new ones, let in the cancer of the truth until the agony could spread from body to mind and destroy a whole world. They were there inside him, urgent to come out, defeat her, silence this woman who was his wife and who had become a stranger. But he held them back because essentially Andrew Keene was a loyal person. He had got to know himself over these last two years, the years of his marriage, as he had never known himself before. And he could remember when Sara had been eighteen, when they had first met. He could understand how she had changed, how the loneliness of a life that should have been a loving state had changed her. He could understand the traumatic effect of losing both her parents at once – even though he could not even remember *his* parents. And he could understand how the claustrophobia of the camp site, the same few people, the same few faces, could make her draw into herself until her husband's face became unfamiliar and even hateful to her. There would still be warm nights when they lay in each other's arms as they had done on their honeymoon; there would still be times when passion would be unleashed in her body and he would find her desire almost uncontrollable. But he could understand too how it was that that side of her had cooled, how the urgency had died, how they rarely even touched. The pregnancy had horrified her, shattered her. Perhaps she would never be the same person again. Perhaps he would never be the same again.

But he could understand. So he kept back the words even though they knotted sourly inside him, wriggling unsatisfied.

Perhaps his thoughts showed in his face for she was silent for a little while. He tried to read, in the faint hiss of the gas mantles. He was not successful; he could not concentrate. Sara sat down and attempted some sewing. It could have been a cosy domestic scene but there was a wall of resentment between them. Neither was aware or prepared to admit its cause but it lay between them.

'We have to move from here,' Sara said quietly.

'I know it.'

'I don't want to return here from the hospital.'

'That's something I can't guarantee, Sara. You surely don't expect me to find a house that quickly? You know what prices are like around here – people coming in, buying up cottages for week-end homes, it's just not possible to raise the sort of mortgage we'd need for something near Stowford.'

'There's Oxford, or Reading.'

'Are things better there?' he demanded.

Her resentment grew.

'You can use that sort of come-back on anything I say. And that's about all you're good for, Andrew – talking, carping, dis-agreeing with me.'

'Is that how you see me?'

'That's how you are! I don't want to keep on at you, I don't want to quarrel all the time, particularly with the baby coming. But you're so ... so *hopeless*. You don't seem to be able to do anything right for us.'

'I do my best,' he replied quietly.

'That's it – you don't do your best. You do nothing, or take the easy way out. Ever since we came here, ever since we got married, I'm the one who's had to do the fighting. Everything that goes wrong, I have to sort it out. You're supposed to be the one who wears the trousers, Andrew, but you don't.'

'That's why you assume them – or try to?'

'What am I supposed to do? If I don't act, things just don't get done!' Sara laid aside her sewing and eased her back against the side of the van. Her face twinged with pain, but her determination was in no sense undermined. He knew she meant to have her say. 'When we came to this site everything was going to be great, wasn't it? Well, I can tell you, I had my doubts from the start. What Lindop told us, it seemed to be too good to be true–'

'You seemed as impressed as I was.'

'But you're three years older than me, and you're the man! You should know about these things – or at least, find out! But I think we were conned. If we buy a van, he said, it would be a good investment. And now what does Ruby tell us?'

Andrew shook his head. 'She's not necessarily got the thing straight.'

'But don't you think you'd better find out? Now?'

'We'll find out when we come to sell the van. There's no point in creating a fuss before that time.'

'And that's always your answer.' Sara's face was reddening with anger again and she leant forward to emphasize her point. 'You always put these things off – until it's too late in the end to get them sorted out.'

'Sara–'

'No, I'm going to have my say,' she interrupted him fiercely. 'It's time you were really told, Andrew. We came on this site and Lindop told us this van was a good investment. And he told us what he was going to do with the site. There was going to be that clubhouse, remember? Six months' time he said. Concrete base already laid. And that's the way it still is – just a concrete base. And then there was the swimming-pool. A place for families to live, he said, fun for the kids. Well, there aren't any real families on the site at all – just a few retired couples, and odd people like Ruby and that man Samson – no kids at all, and for sure there's no swimming-pool, just a damned hole that someone's going to fall into one night and break her neck!'

'You know Lindop explained it was a long-term prospect. All right, it's two years, but the fact is he and Forsyth can't make these alterations to the site unless and until more people are attracted to the site. You can't say it's been a popular site exactly.'

'No, we're the only suckers who seem to have bought here!'

'Now that's not true–'

She brushed his argument aside. 'What is true is the fact that this is no place for us to bring our child up in. And you don't show the right sort of guts that a father should.'

Andrew was silent. He experienced more difficulty now in holding back the angry words, but she was distraught and he had no desire to prolong the quarrel. But Sara was launched into a bitter tirade, as detailed and consequential as it was angry.

'I've had to do all the work in this marriage! Comfort you when you came home tired, and then fight your battles for you on the site! Remember when Lindop was so insistent that you helped level the top end of the entrance – it was I who had to go up there and argue with him, tell him it was his problem and Forsyth's problem not ours and you weren't cheap labour for him!'

Andrew remembered. It had been early on Saturday morning. Chuck Lindop had asked him if he would give a hand with the levelling; he had started, and then Sara had come storming up the site. He could remember her so clearly, standing there, telling Chuck Lindop that they paid to live on the site not work on it. Lindop had pointed out that the work improved the site and they would benefit but she refused to give way. Andrew had stood back feeling rather foolish as Sara argued, but he had seen the way Lindop had looked at her. He had been grinning, not in the least upset, staring boldly at her with an open admiration in his glance. Sara had got even more furious as it was obvious Lindop was hardly listening to her, just staring, and Andrew thought how magnificent she looked – tall, her eyes flashing, *alive*.

Her voice now had a more querulous ring. 'He would have had you cleaning out the lavatories too, if I hadn't put my foot down.'

'It wasn't like that, Sara—'

'It bloody well was! Chuck Lindop tried to make out it was necessary for each of us on the site to spend some time on the cleaning and he suggested we did it by rota. But when I cross-examined him about it, what did he say? The Sharkeys were excused, the Williams family was excused – everyone just about was excused but poor old Andrew Keene. I soon put a stop to that!'

Andrew was silent. He tried to read on, but Sara seemed infuriated by his refusal to argue and her voice rose higher.

'And when there really was something you should have done, something a man *had* to do, what happened? Nothing, precisely nothing. You'll recall what I'm referring to. The shower-room. I told you for weeks I was worried that there was something odd about the room. And you paid no attention. And then I found it. The hole drilled in the concrete blocks of the wall – a *peephole*. What did you do? You *laughed!*'

'Well, it was a bit ridiculous,' Andrew said irritably. 'I mean, it was impossible for anyone to actually *see* anything from that peephole. It gave no real view inside – I suppose a vague view of someone's back, but there's not much to be gained from that.'

'You still miss the point, Andrew! I knew who had drilled that hole – that dirty old

41

man Carter. It wasn't the fact that he could – or could not – see anything. It was the fact that the hole had been drilled there, and that you wouldn't complain to Chuck Lindop about it any more than you'd have it out with Carter!'

Andrew shook his head and laid aside his book.

'For God's sake, Sara, what difference does it make? We couldn't have proved Carter did it, and he left the site shortly afterwards anyway. What was the point of making a fuss? It would get us nowhere and simply cause unpleasantness on the site. It was far easier for me just to cement the hole, and I did that, so what harm was done?'

Sara threw down her sewing with an angry, frustrated gesture. She took a deep breath.

'You simply refuse to face facts. If you don't make a fuss about things that matter–'

'An old man blindly peeping through a hole and seeing nothing of consequence?'

'–things that matter,' Sara repeated firmly, 'things of *principle*, if you don't make a stand about them, where do you end up? You've got to see it from my point of view, Andrew. Even if Carter couldn't see me in the shower, he *tried* to. As my husband, you should have done something about that. All right, so you won't fight your own battles and I fought some for you – I can even accept that. But when you won't even sort out that sort of problem, I despair. I was humiliated, the thought of that old man's cold eyes peering in at me, it gave me the shudders. But you didn't seem to care.'

'Sara–'

'No, let me finish. You've changed, Andrew, you don't seem to care about me and about us any more. You seem to want to opt out all the time. Losing your job, that was bad enough, on top of all these other things, but now over this receipt, you just don't seem to care. In your place, with a wife to support and a child on the way, I'd be *frantic*. Mr Forsyth is up to something, maybe he's going to say we don't really own this van because we can't find the receipt to prove we paid for it, but you seem completely unconcerned. You just want to be left alone, just want to sit there and read your book, in the hope that if you ignore those problems they'll simply go away. But life isn't like that, Andrew. You can't just ignore facts, can't shut your eyes to truth, can't wait and hope and trust that the realities of life will fade away and not bother you. You've just got to face up to things–'

The knot of worms inside him was twisting and wriggling again. He felt anger heat his blood and tried to control it but it was impossible. He stared fiercely at Sara and she stopped speaking. Her mouth remained open, silent, and there was a brief shadow of anxiety in her eyes as she saw the fury that tightened his lips, brought a hardness to his jaw that she had not seen before. The words came thrusting up into his throat so that he grunted, making a physical effort to hold them back as in a wild, tormented fashion justification and pride and despair forced them to his lips. There were so many angry things he wanted to say to her, so many furious, desperate, lashing things he wanted to say, about their life together, about their slide to unhappiness, about the deep, dragging morass into which they were falling. He grunted again, the words there almost like a physical lump in his throat.

'Andrew–' Sara put out a hand, uncertainly, frightened suddenly in a way she had never been before. She half understood, half feared what was happening.

'What...' he gasped. 'What the hell do you *want* from me?'

'Andrew, there's no need to get so ... so upset. You know the way I am, I go on, it's just that I'm pregnant, and things get on top of me–'

'The hell with that! What do you *want* from me, other than silence? Tell me and I'll damn well do it!'

She *was* frightened now. She had never seen him in this condition before, his eyes bright, his mouth twisted, his voice harsh and urgent. She saw his hands gripping the edge of the table and she shook her head.

'When you're calmer, Andrew–'

'No, now!' His eyes glittered as though he were feverish. 'I'm sick and tired of your telling me I'm half a man or no man at all, that I lack the guts to have an argument, that I do nothing, that I'm lazy, that I don't look after you properly, that I'm good for nothing, in bed or out of it. You want me to have it out with Chuck Lindop, is that it? You want me to go up there to his van and face him, have an argument with him, clear the air and say the things you want me to say. Not necessarily what I want to say to him, but what *you* want me to say. All right, I'll do it, because I'm sick of the whole thing, fed up, and mad as hell!'

'He's only just got back to his van,' she said hurriedly, 'you can leave it for a while. Wait until the morning when you're calmer.'

He caught the hint of panic in her voice. It sent the worms wriggling more furiously than ever. 'To hell with that,' he said, almost snarling the words at her. He stood up abruptly, threw his book across the caravan. 'You want me to have it out with Lindop, and I'm going to do just that. And not tomorrow. *Now.*'

He banged the caravan door furiously behind him as he stepped down to the dark, wet grass.

CHAPTER II

1

A light breeze rustled through the trees to his right, leaving a faint sibilant sound on the dark air, like the whispers of long forgotten lovers. At the far end of the field near the entrance from the lane and the roadway, the main lights above the gate, fed from the generator under the hedge, cast bright pools of lights on the gravel track. The dark shapes of the caravans cast long shadows against the light but at the far end of the site, behind him, there was only darkness.

It was down there the clubhouse was supposed to be built, with the swimming-pool at the top end of the slope so that good drainage could be obtained towards the shower-rooms and lavatories in the corner. There were three caravans near the site – Ruby's was one of them – but they were all in darkness. Nor were there any lights glowing in the windows of the vans nearer to him, or up towards the gates. It was as though he, Sara, and Chuck Lindop were the only people on the site. Surrounded by silent caravans, with only the distant hum of a car speeding past on the long straight road some sixty yards beyond the trees, it was like a silent unreal world – just the lights from his own van and those from Lindop's assuring him that life existed here in the field.

His fury and anger were cooling. He did not want to be angry, and yet paradoxically he struggled to feed his annoyance, keep it high, for if he was to face Chuck Lindop without the strength of his anger behind him it would be like all the other times. The fact was, Lindop was a man who could charm the birds off the trees. He had a wicked sense of humour, a capacity to look sideways at things and see fun in them, which was contagious. Andrew could not remember having seen him uncontrolled: even when he had lost his temper there had yet been something at the back of his eyes that suggested his temper was not lost, but merely released temporarily. He was a rogue, a man not to be trusted, his one aim in life was to make as much of himself in as short a time as possible – but there were occasions when he could persuade everyone he was one hell of a fine man.

Andrew did not hate him, though he might have cause to. He disliked him, feared him even, but in spite of everything he did not hate him.

Keeping to one side of the gravel track Andrew walked towards Lindop's van, trying to stoke up the fires that were now dying inside him.

'Andrew? Come on in.'

The words were tinged with a certain relief, as though Lindop had been expecting some other, unwelcome visitor. He had answered the door and his face was dark, suffused with the stain of slowly dissipated anger, but as he called Andrew in it faded. A radio played an Irish air, a greasy pile of paper in the waste bin gave off a fishy smell, and a saucepan of dark brown liquid with the odour of coffee bubbled on the stove.

'Grab yourself a seat,' Chuck Lindop said, 'and join me in a cup of coffee. Couldn't be bothered to make myself a meal tonight, just brought back some fish and chips. The coffee's Turkish though, and if you do get grains behind your teeth, what the hell, it's times like these you family men learn to appreciate what a rough life we bachelors have.' He had so managed to overcome the remnants of his anger that he leered now, winked at Andrew. 'Well, bachelors in name, anyway. Milk? Sugar?'

Andrew accepted the first, refused the second, and received his Turkish coffee in a chipped mug, a present from British Rail. Chuck Lindop held his mug in his hand and took in a deep breath, as though the intake of oxygen would wash out of his system any last traces of whatever it was that had been angering him, and then he sighed. He sat down with a sidelong glance at his visitor; the glance was speculative, as though he was trying to sum up the reason why Andrew might have come here to the van. Andrew's glance slipped away, and Chuck Lindop cleared his throat. He sipped his coffee, pulled a face, reached into the cupboard beside his head and pulled out a flask of whisky. He poured a generous nip into his mug and before Andrew could protest he added some to the second mug also.

'Well, me old son,' Lindop said. 'How goes it?'

He sat there holding his mug in his left hand, his muscular right arm draped along the back of the divan seat he occupied. Chuck Lindop was not a tall man – or at least, he did not give the impression of height, for his body was thick and powerful. He wore a check shirt that was open at the throat and seemed to strain across his chest. The jeans he usually affected on the site were invariably stained and worn; they too emphasized the muscularity of his body. But Andrew's attention, as always, was drawn to Lindop's face. Its most striking feature was the hair that seemed to sprout redly from his nose, his ears and down along his jawline. It was thick, matted, flaming hair that seemed to glow, and in a way it was descriptive of the

49

man itself. Inherently coarse, it gave an impression of strength and virility; it was unruly and wild, and yet could glow softly as satin. Like Chuck Lindop it seemed composed of irreconcilable qualities, and Andrew sometimes fancied it reflected Chuck's moods. It could flare spikily when he was short-tempered; he had seen it soft and tendril-like about Chuck's brow when he had been talking to a woman over a drink. But while Chuck Lindop's hair seemed to change with his mood his eyes never did. They were pale in colour and watchful. They never exposed the man, they lacked expression as a snake's eyes seemed glazed and unmoved. When Chuck was laughing and excited his eyes were still calm; when he was in a rage they remained cool. It was as though they were not part of him, but remained watchful and probing, summing up situations, never panicked, never insecure, never disturbed. They were perhaps the most disturbing thing about the man – they hinted that Chuck Lindop did not exist as a real person. He simply existed as a reflection of the people who surrounded him. Life was one long reaction, the real man would never be discovered, for his motives were buried deep and the surface would never expose them. He took another sip of his coffee and swallowed; his hairy throat was exposed, the red mat of his chest rippling powerfully.

'You not in at Stowford tonight then, Andrew? I thought everyone from the site would be in there for the fun tonight.'

Andrew shook his head. 'No, we couldn't go in really, not with Sara just five weeks off–'

Chuck Lindop clucked his tongue and grinned. 'Ah, well, if you young marrieds will go rushing things, that's what you have to expect. Though I'd have thought a bright young lad like you would have had more sense than to plunge in like that right away.'

He used his disarming smile but Andrew was not disarmed. Where he had found his anger cooling earlier, the embers now flared. He scowled at his coffee mug.

'Mr Forsyth was at the site this afternoon,' he said.

'Oh yeah? What did he want?'

'You.'

Chuck Lindop grinned and scratched his nose. 'Well, Andrew, I'll tell you. I make a point of it never to be around when Jack Forsyth comes calling. Life's pleasanter that way.'

'He pays your wages.'

'Little enough as they are. He hasn't bought my soul.'

'Or your loyalty?'

Chuck Lindop cocked an eyebrow and stared quizzically at Andrew. Lindop's mouth could be brutal; now it was cynically amused. 'Sharp, sharp,' he said. 'You mean you think a man has to be loyal to his *employer?* You'll be telling me to ride a white charger next and rescue Ruby from the bottom of the site and whisk her out of friend Samson's Irish arms. Come on, Andrew, what's bugging you? Got troubles? Ain't we all? You can tell Uncle Chuck all about it, believe me.'

'What's to say my troubles aren't your troubles?' Andrew said petulantly.

'Well, I'll tell you. If anyone has troubles on the site, I regard them as my troubles. Take the lass I just mentioned – Ruby. Now I've known Ruby a few years and she's a good screw, if you know what I mean. I won't deny I haven't been there often enough myself, though I'm not going to make hot dinner comparisons. But she's got her problems; she's maybe told you I moved her down the site, that's true enough, but what she probably hasn't told you is that she's not paid her site rent for two years. She has trouble raising the cash – okay, that's my problem too and I don't push things. See what I mean?'

Philanthropy was the last thing Andrew would have expected from Chuck Lindop and it must have shown in his face for Chuck grinned. 'You can take it any way you like, old son, but I can tell you this. If I used to bed Ruby some time back I don't do it no more. If Hoagy Samson gets in there, that's it as far as I'm concerned. I don't follow on after any wild Irish tinker. It's the other way around; he's the man who takes seconds, not me. I don't pick up crumbs from his table – he picks them from mine.'

It was a situation Andrew had already suspected. Hoagy Samson had been on the site for almost a year and had become friendly with Lindop right from the start. They spent a great deal of time together, in Chuck's van, and drinking in town too, if rumour was to be believed. It was also perfectly clear that Chuck was the stronger, more dominant personality of the two. He was lighter on his feet and quicker of thought; Samson was not slow-witted but he appeared so by comparison with Lindop. To some extent he seemed to want to emulate the site manager, and behaved like a satellite wishing to achieve higher status. But Andrew's impressions were gained at a distance: he had spoken very little to Samson, and knew him not at all well. Once or twice, while he had been at work, Samson had chatted to Sara it would seem, but when Sara had mentioned the fact to Andrew it had been with an element of contempt in her tone. She had even said, on one occasion, that it was the advent of more people like Samson on the site that worried her, made her feel the sooner they left the better.

But Lindop's conversation was diverting Andrew from the main purpose of his visit.

'I really came to talk to you about Mr Forsyth,' he said.

'So what's the problem?'

'He visited a couple of vans before he came to mine. I don't know what he was asking those people, but as far as I was concerned he wanted to know if I could put my hands on the receipt.'

Lindop took a noisy sip of coffee. 'What receipt is that?'

'The one you gave me when I bought the van from you.'

The pale eyes stared impassively at Andrew. There was a short silence as Andrew waited for Lindop to reply, but when the site manager said nothing Andrew blurted out, 'You remember giving me a receipt, don't you?'

Lindop put down his mug carefully.

'You're losing me, old son.'

'What's that supposed to mean? I'm asking a simple enough question. You sold me the van down there for eight hundred pounds. You must have given me a receipt for the money. You do remember giving it to me, surely? And you'll have a copy of your own to show Mr Forsyth.'

'What's Forsyth got to do with it? Is he questioning your ownership or something?'

'I don't know,' Andrew said angrily. 'He

just asked me if I could produce it. I can't. So I'd like to see your copy.'

Chuck Lindop grinned disarmingly. He shook his head, managing to look rueful even as he smiled. 'Well, I'll tell you, Andrew, that's just a little bit difficult. You say I sold you the van. That's not strictly accurate.'

'But you did! When Sara and I came to the site you showed us over the van personally. You told us its real price was eight hundred and seventy pounds but since it was near the end of the season and new models would be coming in you could let us have it for eight hundred pounds, if we paid cash. And that's just what I did – I paid you cash.'

'Not me, Andrew,' Lindop said softly. 'You didn't pay *me*.'

Andrew stared at the confident, red-haired man facing him. His mouth was suddenly dry; he was frightened for some indefinable reason, and the fear drove his anger into a dark corner, left it simmering there. Chuck Lindop drained his coffee, took out the whisky flask again and poured a generous amount into his cup. Once more he added some to Andrew's; this time Andrew hardly noticed.

'I'd better explain the system in all this,' Lindop said easily. 'I took the money from you, sure – but I wasn't selling you the van. You see, when Forsyth put me on this site

the arrangement was that I received a percentage commission on all site owners'
rents, and all overnighters'. That came on
top of the basic, skinflint wage he agreed to
pay me. In addition, if I sold any vans on the
site, I got a rake-off there too. But let's be
clear about this, Andrew. I didn't sell the
vans for *myself* – I simply acted as an agent
for Forsyth. They were his vans, not mine. I
took the money on his behalf, not for myself.
So I wouldn't have given you a receipt, you
see – I mean, would I have committed myself
in that way? It was Forsyth's job to do that,
not me. Besides, even if I had given you a
receipt you couldn't have used it against me,
only against Forsyth.'

Andrew wet his lips. 'That isn't what Mr
Forsyth told me this afternoon.'

The pale eyes were fixed on his. 'Just what
did Mr Forsyth tell you?' Lindop asked
softly.

'He didn't exactly *tell* me, it's more a sort
of impression I gained. He as good as said
he never arranged for my van to come on to
the site at all. He seemed puzzled by the
registration number. He suggested he
couldn't remember ever having seen it on
his books. He did say he had been away for
about a year, after his hernia operation, and
the papers might have been processed then,
but he wanted to see the receipt so he could
check the date and all that.'

'Ahhh,' Lindop said, clearing his brow as though a great mystery had been solved. 'Now I'm getting the picture, Andrew. It's true – I've misled you.'

'You've got a copy of the receipt?'

'Well, no, it's the same situation that I explained to you, except it wasn't Forsyth who owned the van at all.'

'I thought he owned and sold all the vans on this site.'

'He did, in a manner of speaking. But I recall now, about that time he was away with his operation, we were a bit short of vans on the site, the order Forsyth had placed with the coachbuilders hadn't been fulfilled, and I entered into a temporary arrangement with a company from Reading. They brought two or three vans on to the site for me – and it will have been one of *those* vans you bought. I'll have to check, of course.'

'But there were plenty of empty vans on the site at the time,' Andrew protested. 'Why didn't you sell one of Forsyth's to me?'

'Because I couldn't have given you the sort of bargain I offered you on one of Forsyth's vans,' Lindop said in a nothing tone. 'He'd given me no authority to knock off seventy quid; the other people had.'

'Maybe there was another reason,' Andrew said coldly. 'Maybe you got a better rake-off on the van you sold me.'

'That's not a nice thing to say, Andrew.'

Lindop grinned confidently. 'Not a nice thing at all.'

'Either way it makes no difference. I presume there'll be a record of sale by the people with whom you had this *arrangement?*'

Lindop scratched his flaring mop of hair. 'Well, there's a slight problem there. I think they've gone out of business. They were a bit of a fly-by-night firm, I learned later. That's how they came to cut profits and give good discounts. You know, they sort of ignored corners and went right through them. Trouble is, they liquidated suddenly.'

'You mean I can't prove to Forsyth that I bought the van from you?'

'Not from me, certainly – I've explained that. But give me time, Andrew, I'll roust out the name of this firm for you. And don't get so het up, lad. Drink up, and tell me how things are going at the quarry.'

Angrily, Andrew swallowed what was left of his laced coffee. He felt helpless, confused and annoyed. In some way Chuck Lindop was making a fool of him again, laughing at him, spinning him around until he was dizzy with all this talk of distant firms and agencies and financial arrangements. What it boiled down to was that Lindop never had given him a receipt. There was a dim recollection in Andrew's mind now that at the time of the sale Lindop had said the receipt would be forthcoming once his books had been made up – or had he simply given Andrew a scrap of paper naming the price but not stating what the subject of the sale was? Andrew couldn't remember – Chuck had talked so fast and so confidently and had eyed Sara so boldly that Andrew had been overwhelmed, *sold* on the idea of taking the van at a bargain price, and anxious too that he and Sara should get out of the van and away from Chuck's confident, sexual gaze.

Had that been the reason? Was that why Andrew hadn't insisted on a receipt? Or was it simply that he was all Sara said he was – incompetent, bumbling, unable to think straight, easily, so easily *conned?*

Chuck Lindop was talking, talking, talking. He sat there, so confident, clutching his mug of whisky, smiling at Andrew, on top of his world, able to manipulate, pull strings, make people do, say, understand, accept what he wanted them to. Why was it such men could *command?* Why was it that a man so transparent as Chuck Lindop, so *obviously* bent, could charm women and persuade men? He had made a fool of Andrew Keene, that was certain; he had made a fool of Jack Forsyth too. All this talk of firms in Reading was so much eyewash. Chuck Lindop had worked out some fiddle or other to make money for himself and now that Forsyth was suspicious the whole thing was backfiring. But whereas Andrew, in such a position, would have been worried, Chuck Lindop simply didn't give a damn. He was confident he had covered his tracks, he knew he could wriggle away from this situation as he had done from others. He was a student of human nature, a battener upon other people's weaknesses. Upon Andrew's weaknesses.

But Andrew too could turn. He could turn, worm that he was, when he reached the end of his acceptance of life and strike out blindly, unthinkingly. He had done it once, and it could happen again. In the right circumstances.

'I'm sorry to have to ask you, but that's the way it is,' Lindop was saying apologetically, as he leaned forward and slopped the last of the whisky into Andrew's mug.

'Ask me what?' Andrew said in surprise.

Chuck's eyebrows rose and he leaned back against the divan. 'I just told you, Andrew. About moving down the site.'

'What the hell do you mean, moving down the site?'

It came burning out of its corner, the resentment, the anger, the annoyance and the other thing, the part of Andrew that was wounded, bewildered and hurt. He choked on it, unable to speak for a moment, and Chuck Lindop was grinning at him, contemptuously.

'Oh, come on, Andrew. I know I told you when you came on the site that if you bought at once you'd be able to choose your position – and you chose the best one, up under the trees. But I must also have told you that you wouldn't be able to *stay* there. I mean, it's the choicest spot on the site, and I've got two big vans coming on next Monday. They'll be paying twice the rent you are, and I shouldn't think you can match them. If you can, well and good. But otherwise, I'm afraid you and Sara will have to move down the site.'

Sara. The name was an obscenity in Chuck Lindop's mouth. He dared to speak her name. And move them down the site. *Just as Ruby had been moved.* Andrew rose abruptly, an angry tiger growling in his throat.

<h2 style="text-align:center">2</h2>

'You all right, son? You going to be sick?'

There was no solicitude in the words, just contempt. He had made no move; he sat there grinning at Andrew and the bile rose in Andrew's throat.

'You *bastard!*'

'Now go easy, Andy lad, there's no need to carry on that way. You tell me you're short of cash right now and maybe we'll leave it for a couple of weeks. I mean, if it was up to me you could stay where you are anyway. It's not my doing, after all. It's just that Jack Forsyth keeps this place as an investment for his old age, and you can't blame a man for wanting to make the most of an investment, can you? He's got plans for expansion, you see – he intends having the trees cut back, the site opened up a bit, larger vans drafted in, more permanent resident licences, all that sort of thing. Maybe we'll then be able to get on with the clubhouse, and the pool–'

'Clubhouse!' Andrew almost spat the word. 'Clubhouse, pool, receipt, move down the site, you're a bastard, Lindop, and I'm going to break your neck!'

Chuck Lindop laughed. It was a loud, brash, easy laugh that held undertones of real amusement but its surface was scarred with contempt. He rose slowly to face Andrew, still laughing, and he shook his head in a long, slow, swinging movement like a bull bemused by the flashing cloak of a matador. But it was all an act, a cynical, vicious parody of surprise.

'You are going to break my neck? *You?* What with, Andrew? Those thin fingers, those skinny arms, that wide, powerful chest? Are you crazy, son? I could snap you like a twig between finger and thumb. Try laying a finger on me and I'll pick it off like a butterfly's wing. You could no more put the boot in me than you could sort out that wife of yours!

What she wants is a real man, not a milksop like you. It's red blood she needs, a kick up the backside from time to time to shut her mouth and something a bit fiercer at night than you could ever give her. Now *I* could give it to her – but *you?* I've heard her voice evenings, I haven't heard yours. And you say you're going to take me apart? Here, hold my bicep, Andrew, and I'll flex my muscle and break your finger!'

Andrew roared. It was a deep, painful sound born of frustration and fury, issuing out of his chest but the sound seemed only to cause Lindop further amusement. Andrew swung a wild, half-drunken fist in his general direction but Lindop simply leaned back out of range and Andrew half fell over the table. His knees struck the table legs painfully and then he was prostrate as Lindop leaned forward and pushed, open-handed, at his face. Lying on his back, Andrew stared up at Lindop.

Now it was hate, like that other time, the time he tried to forget, deny had ever happened. Perhaps it showed in his eyes for Lindop raised a stubby finger.

'Now just you cool it, Andrew boy, just take it easy and you won't get hurt.'

'Sara–'

'I'm telling you, go easy, don't get excited!'

Andrew struggled to rise, but a foot was

planted in his chest, pushing him back to the floor. He began to mouth obscenities, stupid, childish obscenities as Lindop's red hair seemed to flare in a halo above his head. The light was directly behind him, and Andrew could not see the face of his tormentor but Chuck Lindop's voice came through, smooth and confident.

'Up you get now, Andrew, but easy. A walk in the cool night air will maybe sort you out. No damage done, but don't push your luck, son. You start swinging wild in here, you'll break things up and I won't like that. Here–'

A rough fist seized Andrew by the lapel, jerked hard at him and half pulled him from the floor. He put one hand behind him and pushed up, beginning to rise. As he came up, Chuck Lindop kept his fingers tightly wound into Andrew's jacket. Andrew stood towering above him, four inches taller, but almost like a baby in his hands.

'Dust yourself down, lad, and take it easy. No hard feelings, if you'll cool that temper down. Call it the drink, call it–'

With a *whoomph* the lights above the main gateway went out.

For just one second the two men stood there in surprise. Chuck Lindop was the first to recover. He released his grip on Andrew's jacket and turned to peer out of the window of the van towards the gates. He began to curse, more fluently and more effectively and with considerably more practice than Andrew.

'The bloody generator has blown,' he growled. 'That'll be a packet up Jack Forsyth's shirt. Well, the hell with that, there's not a thing I can do about *that!*'

He turned to face Andrew again just as Andrew swung a half-hearted punch at him. It grazed Chuck Lindop's cheek as the man swayed back instinctively. It certainly did not hurt him, but it brought out Lindop's temper, removed any self-control he had been exercising up to now, and he moved forward swiftly, crouching. His left fist flashed out, his knuckles thudding into Andrew's midriff, doubling him up with an explosive grunt. As his head came down and forward Lindop's blow was transferred into a driving elbow, slicing upwards to meet his face, but catching Andrew just below the chin, painfully in the throat, robbing him of breath and causing him to gasp and choke horribly. Lindop grabbed him by both shoulders and thrust him back against the side of the van. He began to shout but Andrew could not hear the words. There was only the sound, a vague, wild, mouthing of filthy words and names and actions. As his senses cleared some of the words broke through but they were words he did not want to hear and he struggled, trying vainly to strike at the hateful face that was thrust into his, twisted and brutal in its anger.

Lindop took one blow at the back of the neck. He shouted, stepped back, releasing Andrew's shoulder. As Andrew came forward he grabbed him again, swinging him around and thrusting him against the far wall, face forward. Then, before Andrew realized what was happening, Chuck Lindop slammed one fist upwards between his legs from behind, sending pain searing up through Andrew's body. But almost worse than the pain was the hysterical laughter that bubbled out of Chuck Lindop's mouth as the fingers grabbed, took fierce purchase in Andrew's groin and twisted, lifted, until Andrew was on tiptoe, struggling to maintain balance, held painfully, unable to escape his humiliation as Lindop's powerful arm lifted him.

'I'll teach you to take a swing at me, you *schoolboy!*' Lindop shouted. Andrew felt the fingers twisting at him and there were tears in his eyes as he screamed, struggled forward, unable to release himself. Lindop grabbed him by the back of his collar with his free hand and propelled him towards the door, still pulling and twisting at his groin with one hand. 'Next time you come here to see me, you *crawl,* you scum!'

Andrew stood poised in the doorway, arms flailing helplessly as Lindop still held him on tiptoe, laughing almost hysterically at his pain and humiliation. Then with a violent push Lindop released his collar and a fraction of a second later, his groin. Andrew went hurtling out of the van to crash down on the wet grass. He fell on his elbows, skidding forward, and then rolled, fetching up some twelve feet from the van. Chuck Lindop's laughter seemed distant, far away, but the ache in his groin was palpable, insistent, robbing him of any thought but of his body.

Gradually, seconds, long seconds later the pain began to subside. Andrew became aware that he was still lying on his face. The grass was wet under his cheek. He spread his fingers wide, dug them into the soft earth, felt something other than pain again. He raised his head.

The camp was dark. The vans were quiet, no lights showing except in one van, his van, down by the trees. The lights at the entrance gate had gone out and he could see nothing of the gravel path, or the other vans, or the grass more than fifteen feet away. There was no moon, the wind was soft and light on his face.

He sat up, half turning. Chuck Lindop was standing in the doorway of his van, thick and burly against the gaslight. He had donned a donkey jacket and there was a flashlight in his hand. He was about to go up to the generator. He flicked on the flashlight and the beam leapt out into the darkness, playing over Andrew's tear-streaked face, pinpointing his humiliation.

'Get back to your little woman,' Lindop said harshly, 'before I mark your face with something more permanent than a bit of dirt!'

He stepped down from the van, half pulling the door closed behind him. The light from the doorway was cut off, the flashlight played crazily across the grass as Lindop turned away. He was some seven feet from Andrew as Andrew's right hand, levering him upwards from the turf, felt the cold iron against his fingers. The fingers clutched at it, became aware of its weight, cold and hard as the hate in his chest.

He stood up, swaying. Lindop stopped, half turned to look over his shoulder as Andrew moved forward with the heavy iron bar in his hand.

Suddenly, the breeze had died.

3

If you stood at the top of the site just inside the gateway, in the darkness, you could see a faint warm stain in the night sky that was Stowford, lit up with carnival fever. Above the glow the sky darkened, blue and black – black as the trees and the hedge where the furry things rustled their secrets to each other and to the earth that hid them. The soft, wet hush of the grass, the crunch of gravel, the sound of blood pumping in his heart, the cold feel of metal against his cheek. He was becoming aware of the world again, aware of the night and the darkness and the touch of a strip of metal that ran along the side of his van. He had polished that strip in the sunlight until it shone, but that had been an age, a century, a millennium ago.

Someone was crying.

He took a deep breath, tried to stop the sound. He couldn't. He knotted a fist, pressed it hard against his chest, leaned his forehead against the side of the van but the sobs continued.

They were not his sobs.

Andrew stood rigid in the darkness for one long moment, heard the sobbing change to a groan then a subdued, bitten-off shriek, and rushed around to the other side of the van. He threw open the door and almost fell inside. The living area was empty, the gaslight flaring bleakly against closed orange curtains. He pushed against the closed door of the bedroom.

'Sara?'

She was lying on the double bed, in the

darkness, on her side. Her right leg was extended, her left drawn up under her and her body was bowed as though she was trying to relieve the weight of her stomach. As he entered she turned her face; it was a pale blur of pain and fear and anxiety. She turned away again.

'Sara—'

She gave a shuddering sob and then relaxed slightly as he knelt beside the bed. He put out a hand and tentatively she grasped it; her grip became firmer after a moment as though she found strength in his touch. It was a long time since he had felt such reliance coming from her at his touch.

'What is it, Sara?'

'I think it's coming,' she whispered.

Andrew was taken aback. 'You ... are you sure? I mean, it's five weeks yet!'

She was shivering. The spasm of pain had gone and she was relaxing, but she was shivering as though she were cold. Andrew rose, closed the outside door of the van, lit the gaslight inside the bedroom and sat down on the edge of the bed.

'How ... how often is the pain coming?'

As though by way of answer he saw her eyes widen in fear again, felt the tension rise in her body and saw her mouth open as the pain reached up, clawed at her and she cried out.

'*Andrew* ... I don't know ... it's not regu-

70

lar, it comes at intervals, but it's so *sharp*...'

Her hand was gripping his, her fingernails driving into his palm but he hardly felt the pain. He was only aware of the size of her as she lay there, a tall, strong girl, pregnant and frightened. He felt a strength arising in him, a strength he had not felt for years if ever before, but with the strength there was a helpless weakness too. She needed him, wanted his touch – but he was at a loss how to help her.

'Sara, is there anything you need? A hot drink–'

She shook her head. She was calmer, but he could see sweat glistening on her forehead. She still held tightly to his hand.

'It's started, Andrew, I'm sure of it. And I'm scared. I didn't think I'd be scared but I am. Andrew, the pain... But wait, let me think, for God's sake let me think straight.' She was silent for a moment, staring at him earnestly and yet not seeing him. Her eyes held a strange quality, a knowledge he had never seen before. Perhaps its message was one of experience – she was discovering herself, discovering her body for the first time. But her eyes were scarred with cataracts of fear and he knew of no way in which to remove them. 'The phone ... the phone,' she said.

Andrew's mouth was dry. He tried to speak and could not. Her grip tightened on his hand. 'You'll have to phone the hospital,' she said, and stiffened again. 'You'll have to—'

The words were bitten off by a spasm of pain. Andrew leapt upright, squeezing her hand desperately.

'The phone in Lindop's van – it's out of order! I can't go there! I'll have to go up to the road, to Hartley's bungalow, perhaps, but I can't leave you here like this, Sara, I can't leave you, something might happen, something—'

She moaned again, twisting on the bed, and the sound of her agony razored across his consciousness so that he began to shake as though in pain himself. She moaned, rolled on the bed, opened her mouth wide and with one arm fast against her forehead she thrashed around on the coverlet.

'Andrew, for God's sake make it stop… *Andrew…!*'

Her pain made him distraught. He pressed her hand, tried to comfort her, but his own panic was communicated to Sara and she stared wildly at him.

'For God's sake, Andrew, do something!'

Next moment he was saved, as the door to the van was pulled open.

'What's happening?'

It was Ruby.

It was strange how he noticed small things about her. She was wearing a blouse and skirt and the frill at her throat was torn slightly, the blouse loose at the waist. Her hair was disarranged, as though the breeze on the site had pulled at it as she came running down at the sound of Sara's cries. Her face was pale in spite of heavy make-up and her eyes seemed to be sunk in her head, dark marks appearing above her cheekbones like bruises of discontent. She was dressed to go out and yet she appeared drab; she was busy, committed to Sara's pain and yet she seemed to be waiting for something or someone. It was as though she were going through an act, with people watching her, waiting for her to fall from the tightrope, and all the time she was conscious of some danger that would reach for her out of the darkness to pull her down. She was concerned about Sara, yet she was concerned about herself too – on edge, trembling, *anxious*.

But efficient. She busied herself in soothing Sara, got Andrew out of the way to make coffee for the three of them, and then plunged into the back of the small built-in wardrobe to drag out the case and start packing it. When the coffee was almost ready Sara cried out in agony again and Ruby, her eyes sparkling anxiously, came out of the bedroom, grabbed the saucepan from Andrew and almost thrust him out of the door.

'Leave that now. She's in trouble right

enough. Phone the hospital.'

She slammed the door in his face. For just one second Andrew stood there, non-plussed. Then he turned, began to walk towards the gravel path and Sara cried out again. Andrew broke into a run as much to get away from the fear in the sound as to fetch help, for his mind was not yet working sensibly. He was stunned, unable to grasp the situation completely, but he ran, crossed the gravel path and hurried up towards the darkened entrance to the caravan site.

When he reached the lane the breath was already harsh in his chest and he slowed. Fifty yards ahead, where the lane met the main road, an engine roared, the rear lights of a car winked redly as the vehicle pulled away, turning right and driving quickly away, but Andrew paid no attention to it. There was a light in the kitchen window of the solitary bungalow that stood on the corner and he ran for it.

Hartley had a phone. He could phone the hospital from there.

He banged and banged on the door, but for several minutes there was no response. It was as though he was knocking at the door of an empty house, the sound had that echoing note which suggested space, empti-ness, a lack of furniture, but eventually he heard a querulous voice calling and the door opened, with the sound of a bolt being withdrawn.

The door was held on a chain; a suspicious, mean face peered out.

'What do you want? Who are you?'

'Phone–' Andrew gasped. 'My wife – she's having a baby – phone the hospital.'

The face registered surprise, consternation, suspicion in a mixture of emotions that did nothing to persuade him to release the chain. Andrew raised a fist and thudded it against the door in a sudden angry frustration and the man's mouth opened anxiously.

'What the hell you doing? All right, all right, I'll let you in!'

He fumbled at the chain, opened the door and Andrew entered in a rush. He looked around wildly and the little man pointed towards the hall table. Andrew picked up the phone, dialled for emergency services. They answered almost immediately, and the girl's calm, ordered tone brought Andrew to his senses. He wasted no explanations. He gave the address, mentioned the maternity hospital, and asked for an ambulance. It was all over in a matter of seconds.

Andrew put the phone down and looked at the owner of the bungalow.

'I'm sorry if I … disturbed you.'

The man called Hartley just looked at him for a moment. He was small in stature, lean, with a lined, wizened face and knowledge-able eyes. His hair was thin and receding, his manner careful and withdrawn. He was about fifty years old, but he looked older. His skin was pallid, his clothes ill-cut. He wore bedroom slippers that looked fairly new.

'That's all right. You from the site, then?'

'Yes. My wife's pregnant. It's on the way. The phone on the site is out of order.'

The two men stood looking at each other. Andrew felt a reluctance to move, to return to the site even though he knew his duty lay there. He *wanted* to return, but in a sense he was afraid to. Ruby was there, capable; he would be in the way, ordered about, made to feel foolish, a man in a woman's world. He willed Hartley to offer him a drink. The little man made no move.

'The ambulance shouldn't be long, son. They get out pretty quickly.'

'Yes.'

Hartley was standing in the narrow hallway with his back to the living-room door. It was closed, but Hartley gave the impression that any attempt to open it would be resisted with force. There was a nervous aggressiveness about the way he held himself, a determin-ation to repel boarders almost – Andrew considered himself to be getting light-headed at the thought. He was being fanciful, and Sara was in pain at the site.

'I'll get on back then. Thanks for the use of

the phone.'

'Yes. They shouldn't be long now.'

Andrew nodded. Almost instinctively, he glanced at his watch. The hands showed him it was twenty minutes past ten. He frowned. He shook his hand, put the watch to his ear. It had stopped.

'Can you tell me the time?'

Hartley frowned. He opened his mouth to speak, thought better of it. He consulted his own wristwatch. With an odd reluctance he muttered that it had just turned eleven. Andrew thanked him, adjusted his own watch, shook it, and left the bungalow.

He heard the chain being applied to the door behind him.

The ambulance came rushing out through Stowford with blue light flashing and klaxon sounding. It was held up at the crossroads by the gipsy vans that had been parked on the verge contrary to police instructions, but once that particular bottleneck had been passed there was only the narrow country lane to contend with for a couple of miles before the ambulance gained the straight road that would run past the caravan site.

The driver put his foot down when he reached it. He regarded it as a matter of pride that he should maintain a proper timing on all such runs. Stowford was seven minutes; this camp site, he had swiftly calculated as he left the hospital, should take another ten minutes beyond. Certainly no more than that. But schedules could easily be out. He put his foot down and the ambulance sped on, its blue light casting eerie reflections on the trees that lined the highway.

His headlights picked up the painted sign, exactly seven minutes later. He was over time slightly, but it was only a small mis-calculation. There was the sign – *Lovesome Hill Caravan Park* – good name for a preg-nant circumstance. He slowed, signalled, turned right into the lane, and the ambu-lance bumped its way down the narrow lane towards the park entrance on the left.

'No bloody lights,' he grumbled. A rabbit scuttered away with gleaming eyes as he manœuvred the ambulance into the en-trance. The headlights danced down the gravel path. No one seemed to be about; the caravan park was deserted.

'Any sign, Bert?'

Bert peered through the dusty wind-screen.

'There's one light down there,' he said. 'That van over by the trees.'

Even as he spoke a broader shaft of light gleamed against the trees, a van door open-ing at the sound of the ambulance. A dark figure emerged, a tall young man, running, waving.

'Here we are,' said Bert. 'Okay, we'll waste

no time. I'll go in, help the lass out. You can get the van turned.'

'Bit toight, just 'ere,' the driver said. 'Swing round up above, that's the way.'

Bert got out and was hurried towards the van. The driver backed, swung the ambulance around in a long, easy curve. You could never tell on camp sites like these. Once you hit the grass you could easily get bogged down – a bit of rain was all you needed and on a slope like this your wheels could burn a scar on the grass, settle in soft earth and you could be stuck until they brought a tractor to drag you out. Ambulance drivers had to be careful.

He left the engine running and got out. Bert was just coming out of the caravan with the woman. She could walk, but she was obviously in trouble. Her husband was just behind her, carrying a case, looking a bit sheepish. They often did, as though now it was happening they felt they shouldn't ought to have done it in the first place. Bit late now, the driver thought stoically, with memories of his own six ventures in this direction.

He helped Bert assist the woman into the ambulance. The young man got in with her. The pert little bit with the tousled hair and the come-hither figure asked if she ought to go along too. 'Up to you, love,' Bert said, and she looked around the site hesitantly, and decided to stay where she was.

I'd stay, keep you company, love, the ambulance driver thought, if I wasn't busy. He pressed the throttle and the engine roared. Bert rapped on the window to signify everything was okay and the driver swung the ambulance around, heading for the gate.

The pregnant woman – Mrs Keene – she looked close, and taking it rough, first time, he guessed. So he'd take it easy. Hurry, but smooth. Another little pride. First thing, get off this bloody gravel track, great lumps of stone, send the ambulance lurching all over the place. But careful of the slopes, don't get stuck, for God's sake.

Swing left, head slightly for that end caravan, then pull back on to the track to drive out of the gateway. Funny there were no lights up above – asking for trouble, that, with all the gippoes about. Stowford Fair or not, he wouldn't–'

The thought, the complaint vanished from his mind. He slowed the ambulance, stopped. He looked back briefly to see the dark shape of Bert's head, looking forward at him. He put the gears into neutral and sat for a moment staring at the bundle lying just to the left of his headlights. If he had stayed on the gravel track he probably wouldn't have noticed it.

He got out slowly, but his heart was thumping against his ribs. It was one thing to be calm when you handled the sick and the dying on stretchers into the ambulance. It was easy enough to fight the sickness when you'd seen more than a few traffic accident cases being shelled up for the mortuary.

But this was different. He wasn't calm, and his stomach was churning.

'What's up?' Bert called as he got back into the driver's seat. He could trust himself to only a couple of words.

'Police job,' he said, and set out hell for leather for Stowford.

CHAPTER III

1

'Detective Chief Inspector John Crow.'

'Detective-Inspector George Stafford.'

The two men shook hands solemnly, then Stafford gestured towards the car that waited in the station yard, and led the way. 'Good journey?'

'Train was on time, anyway.'

'Down from Edinburgh, hey?'

'Not business. Short holiday, really.'

Stafford slid into the back seat as the driver took Crow's luggage and stowed it in the car boot. 'Didn't think you Murder Squad characters ever managed holidays. Sir,' he added, as a quick afterthought, then caught the gleam in Crow's eyes and grinned. 'Sorry, sir, we're only recently expanded as a force and one gets into the habit of–'

'Don't apologize,' John Crow said. 'I've no objection – we've got to work together so there's no reason why we shouldn't be at ease.' He looked sideways at George Stafford nevertheless. Big, brash, confident, easy in his manners. He'd be a popular man on the force, and one accustomed to getting results. An extrovert who, from his size, would probably have been a striker in the county soccer team or a front row forward in the local rugby club. Young, bright, pushing, perhaps a little impatient. And, probably, right now a little surprised. He'd be thinking that John Crow didn't look like everyone's idea of an efficient Murder Squad man. It was to his credit that he hadn't let the surprise appear in his eyes.

The squad car accelerated out of the station car park and Crow settled back in his seat. 'We've not far to go,' Stafford said, then hesitated. 'You ... er ... you familiar with the area?'

'Familiar enough,' John Crow said. But more than familiar, really. Headquarters were established at Stowford, and that was a village he knew little enough about, but most of the area was reasonably well known to him. In recent years his visits to the Cotswolds had been fleeting, often just a car drive through on the way to another case, but it remained a favourite place for him and Martha, as it had been a magic place for him as a child. It was odd how childhood memories always produced pictures of golden days, but the days he recalled in the Cotswolds certainly were golden. The villages of grey and straw-yellow stone were as mellow as the Cotswold fields of stubble after the harvest, and he could remember sitting with his uncle on a hilltop, being shown the sweeping panorama of a countryside that, perched on the edge of the teeming south-east with its seventeen million inhabitants, was yet medieval in its character. A librarian and local historian, his uncle had tramped John Crow across the awesome vertical western edge of the ancient seabed that had reared up millions of years ago to form the great escarpment. He had shown him twelfth-century grey-walled villages and they had spent long afternoons on the long, open, flat-topped north wolds where the sheep grazed placidly on the high land.

Now, Crow glanced at George Stafford, a local man, and wondered if he had ever seen the countryside as John Crow had. He doubted it. Local people grew up in an area and never saw it – unless there was someone like an uncle of John Crow's to show them. The rounded, heavily wooded hills were just hills; the steeply folded-in coombes just valleys; and the timeless rusticity of the old woollen towns just a stubborn resistance to modern progress, unless you were shown, told, forced to look and see. John Crow had gained much from his uncle, but not only in terms of the Cotswolds. Rather, he had gained an attitude – it made him look at things and people in a way a man in a hurry could not. For the land and people were alike in that one respect – they only gave you their secrets if you respected them, listened to them, *looked* at them. Gave them time. George Stafford would be a man who was short of time. He would say he needed more than life allotted him, to do all he wanted to do. It was an old argument and one John Crow had turned aside from many years ago. Perhaps one day George Stafford would do the same.

'Eggstone,' Stafford said suddenly.

'Sorry?' Crow said, coming out of his reverie.

'Eggstone,' Stafford said, pointing to the distant limestone ridge. 'It's oolite, but around here they call it eggstone because it looks like roe – you know, it's made up of small round granules. I always think that there's no greater stone – you see its sort of honey colour in these buildings?' He leaned forward, peering out at the buildings they passed at the top of the bank. 'Where else in England will you find that kind of stone, hey?'

'Where else?' Crow said, smiling. And where else will you find such a pompous, arrogant, egocentric, supercilious fool as John Crow? 'You must tell me all about it,' he said, still smiling. 'And then we can talk about this man Lindop.'

During the next half-hour John Crow learned a little more about the Cotswolds, and a great deal more about George Stafford. He had been brought up among the tall old stone cloth mills of the Stroud valleys but his father had been a farmer originally and George Stafford looked forward to a similar occupation – on a small scale – when he retired. He was just twenty-six now, satisfied with life, urgent, but not hasty. And he had already done a considerable amount of work on the Lindop murder.

'I've got the files ready for you at the King's Head in Stowford. We thought you'd probably want to work centrally from Cirencester, but an ops room at Stowford is necessary, we reckoned, because of its proximity to the caravan park.'

'I agree.'

'The ops room is set up in Stowford station, and I booked you a room at the King's Head. You can get a good pint there.'

'That helps.'

'Now, as far as the homicide is concerned, we've made a start by taking statements from all the people immediately concerned, including the people who were actually on the caravan site that night, the ones who were in Stowford, the chap called Hartley who owns the bungalow near the site, and the ambulance men, of course. There's been no time to start sifting the statements, but now that you've arrived to take charge the Chief Constable says he'll let us have as many men as we need to get the donkey work done.'

'It looks as though he's having his work cut out in other directions,' Crow murmured as he leaned forward to peer over the driver's head.

George Stafford laughed. 'Everything happens at once.'

They were just entering Stowford. From the top of the hill Crow could see almost the whole of the town. It was typical of many Cotswold villages. It was off the beaten tourist track so had not suffered the birdlands, model railways, aquariums that had been foisted on to places like Bourton-on-the-Water to attract the coaches with their bands of day trippers. It boasted one main street that was broad enough to be called Broadway and held memories of old mailcoaches. Between footpath and road was a wide green strip of turf that was unmarked by parking meters. The houses were honey-coloured, the window frames white-painted, there were hints of Georgian and dashes of mock Tudor, erect, discreet iron street lights, green hanging baskets in front of a scattering of unpretentious guest houses, a tiny hump-backed bridge that was enough to bar motor-coaches, a stream too small to encourage fishermen, a battlemented church that would be no older than fourteenth century and the whole enclosed in a ring of thickly wooded hills that made a newcomer imagine there would be one way into Stowford and no way out.

But right now it was packed.

Parked along the sward right through the centre of Stowford was a long colourful line of caravans. They varied in style from ancient, gaily-painted dilapidation, to heartless cream and chrome. A prominent sign at the first junction denied entry to all cars except on business and in the Broadway itself there were strolling groups of people, sightseers, visitors, locals, mingling with dark-skinned Romanies, swarthy youths showing off ponies, fortune-tellers bangled and complacent about their futures, young girls giggling and hopeful about theirs. In the afternoon sunshine the street gleamed with colour against the bright backdrop of the wooded hills; there was an air of excitement about the place that the local murder would have seemed to do nothing to dispel, and somewhere around a corner pop records blared out a cacophonous chorus that sent ponies dancing in alarm and teenagers jigging in delight.

'Stowford Fair,' George Stafford announced. 'Three hundred years old, they claim, but I've seen records going back only to 1837. But who am I to argue?'

From the window of his room in the King's

Head John Crow looked down upon the throng in the Broadway. He grunted. 'I suppose they'll be kicking up a noise until the early hours.'

'It'll last only another forty-eight hours,' Stafford said. 'Then they'll be packing up. By Sunday the street will be swept clean again. You'll have no trouble sleeping then.'

'Causes problems, though,' Crow said.

'The Lindop murder? Yes. Too many strangers about the place. The local press no doubt will hint that the *coup de grâce* could have been delivered by a Romany hand.'

'Could it?'

Stafford shrugged, and joined Crow at the window. 'It's possible. I mean, we know most of the trouble-makers in this lot. They've been coming for years for the fair. As usual, most of them were in the pubs when Lindop was killed. The problem would be to show some link between a gipsy among this lot and Lindop out at Lovesome Hill. We've certainly heard no whispers so far.'

'Mmm… Well, thanks anyway. I'll get myself a cup of tea and a sandwich, and have a chat with the landlord now, and then I'll come across to the station when I've had a wash.'

'We're just over there,' Stafford said, pointing. 'Almost opposite the King's Head and poised between Madame Defarge and the Count of Monte Cristo.'

When Stafford had gone John Crow rang downstairs and arranged for some tea and sandwiches – he had had no lunch on the train – and then washed away the lethargy that travelling always brought upon him. The late afternoon sun slanted in upon him as he sat down for half an hour and skipped through some of the files that Stafford had left with him. After a little while he rose and went downstairs to his sandwiches and tea, introduced himself to the licensee and his wife, and indulged in a few pleasantries. They were somewhat taken aback by his tall gaunt appearance and their young daughter could not drag her glance away from his bald domed head, but they were soon at ease and amiable, once they had got over the fact of his appearance and the reality of his occupation. Policemen were different, detectives more different, odd-looking detectives most different of all. It was a hurdle John Crow had had to cross all his professional life.

At five-thirty he left the King's Head and threaded his way through the crowded street, passing between the fat woman Stafford had designated as Madame Defarge and the gorgeous middle-aged Romany with the brocaded suit he had called Monte Cristo. The police station beyond was a solid, dark building. Three stone steps, an uninviting façade, an *Enquiries* window that did its best to resist enquiries, and a large room beyond, where George Stafford stood talking to a generously built sergeant and a fresh-faced surly young man in a denim jacket, jeans and high-heeled boots. As Crow entered George Stafford was jerking his thumb in a peremptory gesture and the young man turned disconsolately on his high heels, stared rudely at John Crow almost till he reached the door, and then disappeared into the street.

'Trouble?' Crow asked.

'Not really. Storm in a teacup if you ask me. We've been having the Post Office engineers on our backs for some time – there's been a ham working a local radio around here playing pop music and interfering with the local station that's just been set up. They've not been pleased. Nothing we could do about it because the ham played it very carefully – every time a Post Office van hove into sight he shut down. Until the other night. A fracas developed in the Broadway – a couple of gipsies started waving bottles at each other, the fight spread into Chester Street, and there you are – who should be reporting the battle, hot eye-witness account, but our ham.'

'That was him?' Crow asked, nodding towards the door.

'The very chap.' Stafford's broad face split

91

into a happy grin. 'Course, it was asking for it. I mean, if he wants to become a fight broadcaster he ought to choose a better spot. He'd pinpointed himself for the Post Office people. They were down on him within seconds of his starting the following evening – Chester Street gave up her radio ham meek as modern ale. He's been in this afternoon, arguing. Said when he put out his broadcast at ten-twenty-eight on the dot he was doing a public service, warning the local constabulary of nefarious goings on in Chester Street, preventing a riot and all that.'

Crow smiled. 'What did you tell him?'

'I told him to push off. Argue it out with the Post Office, not me.' Stafford shook his head. 'It was quite a night, though, believe me. A near fatal affray in Chester Street between three drunken gipsies, a tip-off that Northleach Hall had been cased for a likely job, and to cap it all Mr Lindop getting the back of his head bashed in at Lovesome Hill Caravan Park.'

'There are some places with worse records for a night.'

'Yes,' Stafford said, grinning widely, 'but this is *Stowford!*'

They went through to George Stafford's office which was to serve as the operations room in Stowford, and Stafford sat down

92

behind his desk and lit a pipe while Crow began to read through the reports and statements again. Stafford was on his second pipeful when Crow looked up.

'All right,' he said. 'Now tell me how you see this thing.'

Stafford pulled a face. 'This is the first time I've been pulled in on a murder case. I thought I'd be dogsbodying around rather than putting up theories.'

'You're local. You could see things I wouldn't. Maybe you've already seen something. So tell me.'

Stafford laid down his pipe and frowned.

'The act itself was pretty straightforward. Lindop was struck down from behind by a heavy blunt instrument. We picked up a crowbar in the grass; it looks as though it was the murder weapon – there were traces of blood and hair on it – but there's no way in which we're going to lift any prints off it. Anyway, he was struck from behind and it looks as though his skull was somewhat less than normally thick. A muscular feller but with no skull to match. A heavy blow to the back of the head, a good looping swing, and he was a goner.'

'So much for the act. Any confirmations from forensic?'

'Not yet. The reports should be through by tomorrow; all I've been given so far is some preliminary stuff such as I've just given you.

Now then, motive... The going gets tough. No apparent motive. No robbery. Signs of violence inside the van, grass a bit trampled outside, but I'm afraid we've got some clod-hopping coppers and things got a bit churned up out there, so again things don't look too clear. But this Lindop wasn't marked – apart from the hole in his skull, I mean. If there was a bit of a roughhouse inside the van he came off better than the other chap.'

'Until they got outside?'

'Looks like.'

Crow nodded thoughtfully. He crossed his legs at the ankles and fixed his glance on the pale blue socks Martha had put in his bag before they came away. He didn't care for those socks, but he wore them because Martha liked them. A bit of colour to a grey personality she had laughed at him.

'Suspects?'

Stafford tapped out his pipe and thought about filling it again, then reconsidered. He put the pipe in his top pocket and shook his head.

'Stowford Fair draws people from all over the area. There were cars buzzing in to Stowford all through until midnight; the last of the revelry was over by about three in the morning. I suppose almost anyone could have driven from Stowford to the caravan park and smashed Lindop's head in.'

'What about the people on the site?'

'Almost everyone was in Stowford, it seems. Lindop was on the site after an evening in Stowford – he was seen drinking with some acquaintances in the Miller over the way at about eight in the evening. But he must have been back there at the site about nine-thirty. The only people left in the vans at that time were a married couple. Chap called Andrew Keene and his wife. She was in labour. A daughter was born next day, prematurely – intensive care unit right now.'

'What's Keene like?'

Stafford shrugged. 'Tall, thin, kind of dreamy – we're looking into him. He's made a statement up at the hospital today. So has his wife. We're running a check on both of them, and on Lindop too, of course.'

'Who owns the site – I gather from the files Lindop was site manager?'

'That's so. Chap called Forsyth owns the place. Says he's going to close it down now – been unhappy about it for some time. It would seem he was out at the site the afternoon before Lindop got smashed. He was looking for his site manager. The Sharkeys – a couple who live on the site – they say he wasn't too pleased with Lindop.'

Crow raised his eyebrows, wrinkling his domed brow. 'It's a start, anyway. All right, now what about this generator thing?'

George Stafford scratched his head. 'Not

something that seems to fit, somehow. It looks as though someone blew the generator–'

'Explosive?'

'Dynamite. Just a little – enough to knock the generator apart and fix the lights above the gateway for good. But why was it done? Keene reckons he heard the explosion about ten o'clock – which would probably be *before* Lindop was killed. But why blow the lights, then come down, have a scrap with Lindop in the van and do him outside with a crowbar? I mean, there was no one on the site but the Keenes and there must have been a quieter way of going about things than blowing a generator.'

'Did Keene go out to investigate?'

'No.' Stafford hesitated, seemed about to go on but thought better of it. Crow waited a moment but did not ask him further – if Stafford had something on his mind it was as well to wait until he thought it ripe enough to come out. Crow nodded, uncrossed his legs, stood up.

'Fine. So let's get to work. I want you to chase up the file on Lindop and the others, try to get forensic to put their skates on, and if you can find out where the dynamite used to blow the generator came from, it would be helpful. Any quarries nearby?'

'The disused one south of here – Horse Bottom, or as they say locally 'Arse Bottom

96

Quarry – and then the two up near Fox-holes.'

'Try the Foxholes quarries. It's a good enough situation to start in. As for me, I'm going to do a bit of sightseeing in the Cotswold countryside.'

'You're going out to Lovesome Hill?'

'As they say,' Crow agreed gravely, 'to view the scene of the crime.'

2

There would be nothing to see, of course. The local police would have combed it, the forensic people would have picked over it, the site-dwellers would have satiated their curiosity over it, and there would only be a trodden-grass area around the screens erected by the police when the body was found. Nor was there any *atmosphere* to be picked up – John Crow had long ago learned that the *frissons* that the scene of a murder could give were subjective issues only. They were impressions he had learned to distrust because they came from inside, they were not external evidence. With people it was different; a man could learn a great deal from the impressions that people made upon him. Learn about them, and learn about himself too.

The last cottage on the outskirts of the

town possessed an overflowing rose garden whose blooms were scarlet against the mellow stone of the wall; Crow leaned back and half closed his eyes. It would do as an image to retain until he had to face stark realities again, like blood, and bone splinters, and death.

Five minutes later the police driver said over his shoulder, 'About another half-mile or so, sir.' Crow opened his eyes and looked about him. Stowford had disappeared in the hollow of the hills behind and the squad car was moving along a straight road that crossed the hill and dipped into a slow slope beyond. From the hill he could see in the north distance a low limestone ridge, patchwork fields, clumps of woodland and winding valleys. Nearer to hand a half-mile stretch of tree-edged road and the farmhouse to the right, about a mile off the road, the squat bungalow fronting the road at the edge of the lane. Between and beside the two buildings was a sprawl of cream-dotted green – Lovesome Hill Caravan Park.

The thought of a caravan park in the Cotswolds would be pleasing to some; to John Crow it was distasteful. He had seen the way these caravans blighted the coasts of the south-west, and if the same happened to the Cotswolds the area could change overnight. But as the police car drove on to the Lovesome Hill site Crow had to admit it had its attractions. The belt of trees screened the site from the road, there was a nakedness about the area that was green and pleasing, there were only about twenty or thirty vans on the site and a number of them were unsold. Life could be quiet and pleasant here, he thought – if you like that sort of thing.

He told the driver to stop near the gate, and then he got out and walked down the site, a tall, gaunt, bony figure with a long stride, slow and determined. He approached the car parked near the first van, glanced at it, passed it and walked towards the small worn area where pathologist and policeman had worked.

It looked innocent enough now.

There was nothing to be seen, of course, nothing significant. But it gave John Crow a picture of the scene where the murder occurred, and things like this could help. He was still standing there, looking about him, when he heard movement in the van at his back. He turned.

The man standing in the entrance of Lindop's van was short and thickset, almost bald, angry, frustrated, and upset. He was glaring at Crow from beneath strips of bushy eyebrows and his hands were stuck deep in his pockets.

'Good evening,' Crow said.

'Another policeman, I suppose. Or a

reporter.' The speaker looked again at Crow and obviously settled for the former description. Crow introduced himself.

'My name's Forsyth,' said the little man aggressively. 'I own this site – and it's brought me nothing but trouble. To hell with it now, I'll close it down as soon as you people get out of the bloody way.'

Crow paced forward, hands behind his back. He looked carefully at the van.

'Your site manager lived and worked in here?'

'That's right. Served as an office, and he lived here as well. 'Bloody good, easy job if you ask me. But that wasn't enough for him, was it?'

'Wasn't it?'

Forsyth snorted. 'You got the bloody books, haven't you? I came along when I heard Lindop had been ... murdered...' He hesitated, almost eschewing the word and then hurried on. 'But by the time I arrived your people had taken over the van, looking for fingerprints and all that nonsense, and they took Chuck Lindop's papers and books too. Well, you can tell *me* what fiddles he's been up to.'

Crow shook his head. 'I can't tell you yet because I haven't inspected the books. Er ... shall we go inside?' When, after a momentary hesitation Forsyth stepped back into the van, John Crow followed him, looked around the interior with a certain interest, and then smiled. 'Now, you were saying … fiddles? Just what had Chuck Lindop been up to?'

Forsyth looked around him distastefully, as though Lindop's depredations still stained the caravan. 'Like I said, I can't be sure because I've not gone through the books he kept, but I got a pretty good idea what he was up to. I been talking to the people on the site, and it looks as though he was fiddling me all right. Maybe it was my own fault for not keeping a tighter rein on him, but he was a bloody slippery customer, you know, and he could be … *persuasive*.'

'So what was he up to?'

'Well, he was *supposed* to keep a record of overnighters and pay me the rent, keeping a commission for himself. From what I gather from the Sharkeys, there was never a lot of people stayed overnight, but there were certainly more than I got paid for. Now that's small beer, and it doesn't bother me too much. I lose, but it's the permanents I'm more concerned about. And that's where he was really milking me, I suspect.'

Crow frowned. 'How could he not declare rents from permanent site residents?'

Forsyth shook his head glumly. 'That isn't the problem. I been looking at all the empty vans on the site. Some of them tally, some of them were brought on, okay. But there are two that don't.'

He looked at Crow expectantly. Crow stared back, then shrugged. 'I'm sorry, I don't see the point.'

'I have an arrangement with a firm in Oxford,' Forsyth explained. 'They sell me vans at a fixed price. I sell those vans here on the site: buyers pay for van plus site, which gives me a nice profit. If they want to leave the site they can, taking the van with them, for a further fixed fee. That leaves room for a new van, and a further sale for me. At least, that's the way Lindop was supposed to work it.'

'And he didn't?'

'Damned right he didn't. It seems he worked two fiddles. One was to insist on an option to purchase the van at his own, low price – he did this to a couple of people, retired chap called Orton, for instance – and then sell the van *off* the site, second-hand, at a higher price. The other fiddle is the one that really gets my goat. He'd fixed up his *own* arrangement, as far as I can gather, with a van company. A fly-by-night firm, I think, not too much bothered about ethics, maybe they even pinched the vans themselves in the first place, I don't know, I've not been able to check on them, anyway. But the system was that Lindop bought vans from *them* as a site fell vacant, put that van on and sold it, and never told me what was happening. In other words, Lindop was taking the rake-off that should have been coming to me as site owner.'

Crow nodded thoughtfully. 'Did you speak to him about this?'

'Didn't have the chance. Been suspecting it for some time, but each time I came out to see him he just happened not to be around.'

'But you spoke to some people on the site the day he died.'

The bushy eyebrows drew together as Forsyth considered the implications behind Crow's first statement. He teased at his lower lip with a yellowing dog-tooth. 'Well … yes, I did. That's how I got the pieces of information I'm giving you now. And a bit more.'

'How do you mean?'

'Have you spoken to Andrew Keene yet?' When Crow shook his head, Forsyth grinned maliciously. 'It looks as though I wasn't the only sucker around here. That Keene lad, he's pretty soft and pretty green. All right, Lindop was swindling me, and if I'd had proof before he got killed I'd have shot him off this site at a rapid rate of knots. Come to that, I've still not got the *proof*, not until I've seen his books. But young Keene, maybe he can raise some proof for us. You see, he can't *prove* the van he's living in was his.'

'He bought it from Lindop?'

103

'So he says. But he can't produce any piece of paper to say so. And where does that leave me? I'll have to go to law about it, for an opinion, but it seems to me that if the Keenes are living in a van on my site and they can't prove they paid good money for it, I'd be entitled to reclaim the van.' He squinted suspiciously at Crow. 'Wouldn't you see it that way?'

'I'm not sure I would. I don't know all the facts.'

Perhaps something of Crow's feelings showed in his face, for Forsyth said defensively, 'I'm a businessman. This site is an investment. Lindop's been bleeding me, and I can't afford to be sentimental about these things.'

'Did you ask Keene about his receipt?'

'Spent an hour or so with him while he looked for it that afternoon. If you ask me, it never existed. A dreamer, that lad, doesn't know whether he's coming or going.'

'I presume he was worried about the matter?'

Forsyth shrugged. 'Suppose so. But his wife – she wasn't worried, she was hopping mad. At me, maybe; but more at him. Her husband.' He paused reflectively. 'I reckon she'll have given him a good roasting that evening.'

The Keene caravan was empty and locked.

Crow was tall enough to be able to look through the wide end window which gave a prospect down along the site to the sloping farmlands beyond, and the interior of the van looked homely, tidy, clean. There was a copy of the *Guardian* on the window seat, and a paperbacked book with a lurid cover beside it. He tried to read the title, but was unsuccessful. He stepped back away from the van towards the trees and looked across towards Lindop's van, where the body had been found. The site was the last one before the gate some thirty yards beyond, and set in a direct line with the lane, effectively barring access to anyone who entered the site. No one could come on to the caravan park without passing the Lindop van.

He turned, looked down towards the far end of the site, past the empty vans to the lavatory block and the small cream caravan parked near it. There was a woman in the van; she was sitting there, looking out, staring at him. He stared back, and after a long moment she rose, disappeared, only to come into sight at the corner of the van. She stood there hesitantly for perhaps five seconds, and then she walked up the site towards him.

Crow observed her as she walked towards him. About five feet and a bit, rather stocky, a provocative walk with swinging hips, a woman who knew her way around. A lively face and a wide mouth; carefully set hair; a body clothed with deliberation and little else – or at least, as little as possible. She stopped some ten feet away from him, and looked him up and down coolly, but Crow guessed she was far from cool inside. This was an attempt to calm her own nerves, tell herself she wasn't worried. He wondered what she had to be worried about.

'I saw the others yesterday,' she said, 'working over the van. Fingerprints, all that stuff.'

'Yes?'

'Made them some coffee.'

'Kind.'

The china blue eyes held his for a moment, then she grinned as she caught the twinkle in his glance. 'You like some?'

'That would be pleasant.'

She gestured down towards the small van and turned away. Crow followed her, feeling slightly absurd, aware of his height and boniness in a way he rarely was these days. It was just the incongruity in their shapes – she was round and short and bouncy, while he was all bone and angularity. He had to stoop to enter her van; she already had her coffee percolator boiling away merrily.

'My name's Ruby,' she announced. 'Ruby Sanders.'

'John Crow. Detective Chief Inspector.'

'You was looking at Andrew's van,' she accused him.

He admitted guilt.

'He's at work,' she explained. 'Up at Foxholes – he's in charge of the stores up at the quarry when he's not tearing off to see his wife in the hospital. You'll have heard she just gave birth to a daughter. Caesarean.'

'I had heard.'

She turned aside and poured him a cup of coffee. She handed it to him, offered him milk and sugar, then took a cup herself. She eyed him soberly. 'Saw you talkin' to old Jack Forsyth. Don't want to pay heed to everything he goes on about. If he said something nasty about Andrew Keene...'

She let the statement die away, almost a question. Crow made no attempt to fill the void in the conversation. He sipped his coffee.

'Did Forsyth tell you to have a word with Andrew?' she tried again.

'He said there might have been certain problems,' Crow replied non-committally. 'But I shall want to speak to everyone on the site personally, in any case.'

'You've already got statements.'

'That's so. But it helps to talk. People ... remember things.'

I bet, she was saying with her eyes. When you sit down and start digging into their minds I bet they remember things. Aloud, Ruby Sanders said, 'Chuck Lindop gave most people problems, of one kind or another.'

Crow smiled. 'What problems did he give you?'

Ruby hesitated. She sipped her coffee, looked uncertainly at Crow, took another sip and then put her cup down. She reached for a pack of cigarettes, lit one, sat down in the window seat and swung her legs up under her. Defiantly, through a haze of blue smoke, she tossed her head. Her hair, thickly lacquered, swayed in its styling but gave no sign of collapsing.

'No reason why I shouldn't tell you,' she said. 'I'm a grown girl, and responsible to no one but myself. And if I don't tell you, there's sure to be some creep around who *will* – and then you'll come back and say why didn't I tell you in the first place? So what the hell. Thing is, Chuck and I had something going for a while.'

Crow sipped his coffee and said nothing. Ruby inspected the glowing end of her cigarette as though she had seen nothing like it before. A slight frown marked her brow as though she were looking for images that were suddenly difficult to find. Perhaps remembering a love affair with a man who was dead was more difficult than recalling one with a person she could still see on the site.

'They weren't bad days,' she said reflectively. 'No, hell, they were good days. Chuck could be a lot of fun. When he put himself out to please a woman he could do it, believe me. I'm easily pleased, of course – but Chuck was something again, I can tell you. Why he–' She broke off with a quick darting glance at Crow, as though wondering whether she should go on at all, and then she shrugged. 'To cut a long story short, when I came on to the site here there was a flash Harry running the place who didn't know his backside from his mouth and then old Forsyth bought up the place and installed Chuck Lindop as manager. First thing Chuck does is come around for a cup of coffee, just like you, now, and within thirty minutes we was in the sack–'

She stopped again and Crow grinned at her. She saw the humour in the situation and grinned back, relaxing somewhat.

'Well,' she said, 'I told you, he could really please a woman when he set out to. Not that I'm suggesting... Anyway, after that we had a going thing, you know? Maybe six months. But, like lots of other fellers, he got tired, maybe it's the way I yammer, maybe it's because they see me with a couple of brandies inside me and my hair down some night, I don't know what it is, but like the others, he decided that was it. You know what I mean?'

Crow nodded, watching her. She was past the first flush of youth and with it had gone much of her innocence. Even so, he suspected that her cynicism was still edged with hope, she would still expect that one day things would be different – were already different, for all he knew.

'I know what you mean,' he said quietly.

'Ahuh ... Chuck, now, I'll say this for him, he was this much different from the other characters I've known. Couple of them, they've given me the old heave-ho and you'd think I was something crawled out of the wainscoting next time I spoke to them. Chuck wasn't like that; he gave me the push, told me so, in fact, right out, took my breath away so's I couldn't yell at him – but he didn't just cut me dead thereafter. We stayed friendly. It was all right. I was a bit mad, I admit that, but we was still on speaking terms. It was just he'd found some other woman to crawl into the sack with – could I complain about that? We weren't married, for God's sake.'

'Lindop ... ah ... played the field then?'

Ruby's face creased into a broad grin. She shook her head, almost ruefully.

That's an understatement. When he wasn't with me, he was with some other bird. And after we finished, I don't reckon his appetite changed much. Now look, talking to a copper is like talking to a doctor, you know, so I can tell you. Chuck was good in bed – and he saw no reason why lots of women shouldn't know. A woman to Chuck

Lindop was like a … well, you hold up a target, he had to let fly an arrow. Know what I mean?'

'How long was it since you and he separated?'

Ruby shrugged. 'Eight months, I reckon.'

'Was he dating someone recently?'

'Bet your last quid on it.'

'Who was it?'

Ruby pulled a face and shook her head. 'You'll have to ask around. I've stayed out of Chuck's way since he moved me down the field.' The uncertainty was back in her china blue eyes again. 'You'd better know about that, too. I didn't play the rules with Chuck. When he'd finished it should have stayed that way. But I still … well, I lusted after him one night when I got a bit canned, and I went over to his van. Just walked in on him with my best see-through negligee – you know, film star stuff? He almost threw me out.'

'Another woman with him?' Crow asked.

'No, no – a man, as a matter of fact. But next day he came around and told me I'd have to move down the site, well away from him. I didn't argue.'

'Not such a good position,' Crow murmured, looking out of the window. 'I'd have thought you would have complained.'

Ruby hesitated. 'He had a look in his eye.'

Crow nodded. There was a short silence.

111

He finished his coffee. 'I've read your statement,' he said.

'That Inspector – Stafford? When *he* read it, he said it wouldn't be easy to check out. I don't see why. I was in the George and Dragon that evening – couple of dozen people can verify that.'

Crow looked at her soberly. 'But as far as I recall, you left the pub at about nine.'

Sincerity and earnestness oozed out of Ruby's eyes. 'But I *told* you coppers what happened! I was in the George and Dragon and there was this feller – he was called Jimmie – he picked me up, told me he was a commercial traveller, and I didn't want to stay around those pubs when all those roughneck gippoes was about. So I let him persuade me. We left about nine, we had another drink at the Hammer, and then he drove me out here to the caravan park. We stopped at the end of the lane, he pushed off, I came on to the site – and dark as hell it was too – and I heard the screaming. I went over to the Keene van, and there they were–'

'This man – Jimmie. He gave you no other name?'

'No.'

'It's just that we can't verify your story from nine until the time you arrived at the Keene van,' Crow explained. 'What time was that?'

Ruby frowned, and a tiny line of uncertainty seemed to flicker in her eyes. She shrugged. 'Can't be sure.'

'Try.'

'Can't be *sure!* Some time after ten-thirty, I reckon. Maybe ten forty-five give or take a few minutes either way. Ask Andrew Keene – not that he'll be too sure, I guess, since he was worried as hell about his wife. I sent him packing almost immediately to phone for the ambulance. *They* arrived bang on eleven-fifteen, I can tell you that 'cos I looked at Sara's watch just about then.'

'Was there a light on in Lindop's van?'

'No. I told you – it was all dark. And like I said to Inspector Stafford, and wrote in the statement – I didn't hear anything either. All I heard was Mrs Keene moaning with the pain – and they had to operate on her in hospital, you know that?'

Crow nodded. He waited, but Ruby seemed disinclined to say any more. She seemed to feel insulted that he should have asked her the last few questions. She wasn't a suspect, was she? The question was there in the angry pout of her mouth. John Crow rose to go. He thanked Ruby for the coffee, had almost reached the door when she said: 'One more thing.'

'Yes?' Crow said, turning.

The defiance was there in her eyes again. 'I told you about Chuck because the noseys on

113

the site would probably have told you anyway. So I might as well get it all off my chest. If they talk about Chuck, they'll talk about others too. You'll hear from them about Hoagy Samson, so I'll tell you first.' Her chin came up, daring him to disapprove. 'Hoagy came on the site about nine months ago. He took up with me a month after Chuck dropped me. We still sleep together occasionally. All right?'

'But he wasn't with you that night?' Crow asked.

Her eyes widened suddenly and she sat up. 'You'll have to ask him where he was. Last time I saw him he was in Stowford with some gippoes. But Inspector Stafford promised he wouldn't tell Hoagy, or let it out that I got a lift home from this Jimmie feller that night. You won't let on, will you?'

Crow shook his head. 'I won't let on.'

As he left the van a little dog with a patch of black over one eye came dawdling along, smiling at him.

3

'Hogarth Samson,' Inspector Stafford said heavily, and tossed the file on the desk in front of Chief Inspector Crow. 'He's got form, all right.'

'Tell me.'

Stafford dropped his mouth like a dolorous bloodhound and sniffed. 'Nothing very big, nothing very important. He's a roughneck, is friend Hogarth. Never held down a job for long, worked as a brickie's labourer over on the Shenstone site last summer and made a few bob. Picks up some money on the horses from time to time – he's got a lucky streak for such a thickie. Still, maybe he deserves that, for having parents who'd saddle him with a name like *Hogarth*. We've had him inside more than a few times for drunk and disorderly; couple of assault cases. We think he's had his hand in some petty thieving, a bit of receiving too – but we've pinned nothing on him so far. But we don't *like* him. He's big, he's awkward, he's ugly and he's belligerent. One of these days he'll lose his temper – and he's thick enough to go too far, clobber some-one, and find himself up for something big.'

'As big as Chuck Lindop?' Crow asked softly.

'Could be. But Hogarth is a man of habit. Right now, for instance, he'll be in the George and Dragon. A regular patron. Studying form for the first race this after-noon, over a pint. And most evenings he's there swilling with the lads. As he claims to have been the night our friend got ham-mered.'

'The George and Dragon, you say?' Crow

smiled. 'I could do with a pint myself.'

The bar was crowded. Stowford Fair might be staggering on its last legs now but there were still more than enough tipplers to fill the George and Dragon at lunchtime – regulars, sightseers, and a group of swarthy men from the Romany vans scattered the length of the Broadway. They seemed more sensitive than most to the presence of a policeman; Crow became aware of a number of dark eyes flicking glances in his direction as he pushed through the throng to get to the bar for a pint for himself and one for Stafford. It could have been that they were surprised by his physical appearance, but he doubted that. Policeman. It was there in their eyes.

Crow got the drinks, called Stafford across and they stood at the corner of the bar, backs against the wall, and looked around.

'Over there, in the far corner by the window,' Stafford muttered and sank a copious draught of beer. Crow watched him in astonishment, and Stafford grinned. 'Long practice. Pubs is great places for information, and a chap looks odd if he chats in a pub and doesn't drink.'

Crow took a less hefty drink himself and then allowed his glance to drift casually towards the window seats. It was not casual enough, for the big man with the curly hair and the donkey jacket stared straight at him and grinned. He leaned sideways, said something to the man on his right and they both laughed. A quick conversation, and then they rose, elbowing their way past protesting acquaintances. The big man led the way towards Crow.

'You was lookin' at me, so I guess you wanted a chat, hey?'

Crow sipped his beer and looked coolly at the two men facing him. 'One of the problems of being a policeman is that I can't choose the people I have to speak to.'

The man with the curly hair reddened. He had his arm over his companion's shoulder; the grip tightened.

'I don't *have* to speak to you,' he said.

'But you do,' Crow replied. 'I didn't invite you over here. But you're Hogarth Samson, and you *need* to talk to me, to convince me you had nothing to do with the death of Chuck Lindop.'

Samson's mouth was twisted unpleasantly and his eyes glittered as he glanced from Crow to the amused Inspector Stafford. 'You suggestin' I *did* knock Chuck on the head? In front of a witness?'

Crow shook his head slowly. 'I'm quite prepared to take a statement from you if you want to admit to it, but I'm not suggesting you did it. As for a witness, I imagine your … ah … friend here is with you because he

117

has already been a witness to something.'

The man with Hoagy Samson looked baffled, his close-set eyes flickering uneasily at his nearness to two policemen. He was a gipsy, policemen were his natural enemies, and alone he would never have dreamed of crossing the bar floor to speak to Crow and Stafford. But Samson's arm was across his shoulders, and Samson's fingers were digging into his arm.

'I was with Hoagy,' he muttered. 'That night, me an' Hoagy was here, drinking.'

Crow nodded. 'I'd heard.'

'We've got it written down too,' Samson said harshly. 'It's there in writin', me an' Billy here was in the pub all evenin', till throwin' out time. So there's no way you can tie me in with bashin' old Chuck over the head. That's right, hey?'

'So what are you so anxious about?'

Samson stared at Crow. His earlier belligerence had faded to be replaced with a cautious truculence. He considered his answer for a little while.

'I know you coppers,' he said at last.

'Rather better than you should do, I understand,' Crow replied.

'If I been inside a few times, that don't mean I'd take a crowbar to Chuck Lindop!'

'No, but it does suggest to me that you might be aware of the person who might have done it,' Crow said. 'I gather you knew

Lindop fairly well, visited him at his van, went out drinking with him from time to time.'

'We was friendly.'

'Sometimes a man with friends doesn't need enemies.'

'Oh no.' Samson shook his head. 'I had no cause to quarrel with Chuck. And I don't know who did. Come to that, even if I did I wouldn't grass to you – or any of your kind.'

'You'll be telling me there's honour among thieves next,' Crow said.

'Now look here–'

'What about you, Billy?' Crow said, ignoring Samson's threatening tone. 'Anything to add to what you've said in your statement? You and Samson *were* here all evening?' The gipsy licked his lips. 'We was here – and down the road at the Miller. Took a skinful, I did, but me mind's clear as a bell and me memory's prodeejus when I've had a few beers and I'm with me muckers.'

'Like me,' Samson said, glowering.

'Thass right. Like Hoagy.'

The two glared defiance at John Crow, who smiled non-committally. Away from Samson, Billy the gipsy would no doubt be much less certain and far less belligerent in his relationship with the police, but he borrowed truculence from Samson and was able to raise a defiant chin. As for Samson, he *seemed* tough enough, but John Crow suspected he

119

still lacked inner strength and confidence. The man had been friendly with Chuck Lindop; it was said he tried to emulate him, be as positive as the dead man in his attitudes. Perhaps Hogarth Samson had got into trouble over the years because he had been trying to prove himself to himself; now Lindop was dead there was the possibility he saw himself stepping into Lindop's shoes. The unanswered question so far was – how had Lindop filled those shoes?

George Stafford came into the office later that afternoon with a pleased smile on his rugged face. He waved a report and dropped it on Crow's desk.

'Bit of a lead at last.'

'What's that?'

'Foxholes Quarry. Sent a constable up there, do some checking. They've been through the stores and looked through their explosives book. Sure enough, there's a shortage on the dynamite list. Someone's been lifting a few sticks.'

Crow frowned. 'Is that the quarry where this man Keene works?'

'That's it. He's in charge of the stores there.'

'Could be little more than a coincidence, of course. He lives at the site, he was there the night Lindop died, and he works at a quarry that's lost some dynamite – but we don't yet know *why* the generator was blown at the site. Apart from that, though I haven't interviewed Keene yet, everyone tells me he's a bit dreamy, quiet chap–'

'Aha!' Stafford said importantly. 'It only goes to show, though, doesn't it – you can never tell about these things.'

'And just what is that dark comment supposed to mean?'

Stafford sat down, enjoying himself. 'You'll know better than most that you can't tell a chap by the way he looks.' He paused then, somewhat at a loss as he found himself staring at Crow's bald head, deep-set eyes and hawkish nose, and aware of the implications behind his statement. 'Well, what I mean to say is, young Keene is a quiet enough chap, sort of dreamy even, and the story he's put about is that he's working at the quarry because he was made redundant in his last job, the one he was holding since before he got married. Now then, I have information which tells me otherwise.'

'Tell me.'

'We've started checking all the stories given in the statements now, of course. I've also got those two men you detailed to check backgrounds giving me reports every time they come up with something. Well, one of them comes up with a story about Andrew Keene. He was well thought of at the firm he worked for – he was a clerk in a haulage firm working out of Northleach. Been there for about four years, it seems. Well, he got married, and everything was okay for a while, then almost a year ago he began to get moody and depressed, his work fell off, and the boss – chap called Clarke – had to speak to him several times.'

'You're saying Keene was dismissed for incompetence, not on account of redundancy?' Crow asked.

'No, not at all! Keene got into hotter water than that. Clarke wasn't too happy about the way he was doing his job, and it may be he was looking for a chance to give him the push anyway, but Keene gave him one on a platter. There was one of the drivers, a fellow called Baker, one of these big, loud-mouthed bullies, whose particular pleasure it was to take a rise out of Andrew Keene. Every time he passed Keene's office he'd stick his head in, start ribbing him, give him a bit of a going-over verbally. Keene didn't seem bothered, just ignored it. Until one day Baker met Keene down at the loading bays.'

'The worm turned?'

'And *bit*,' Stafford said with a grin. 'I think from what I'm told more than a few people were pleased, but what happened was that Andrew Keene went for Baker with a piece of chain he'd picked up from the floor. Caught him across the nose, broke the bone, sent blood all over the place and Baker was screaming like a stuck pig when they hauled young Keene off him. Clarke had young Keene in, but got no satisfactory explanation, so told Keene he wasn't satisfied with his work and this was the last straw – he couldn't have that sort of violence among the workers. He gave Keene the push.'

'Did this man Baker prefer charges?'

Stafford shook his head. 'He was happy enough to leave it there. I suppose he was shattered by Keene's reaction. And the fact it was he who ended up on his back, bleeding, wouldn't have helped his ego. No, he up and left too, went up north. Clarke says he was last working for a haulage firm in Doncaster. But you get the picture as I see it?'

Crow smiled. 'How do you see it?'

Stafford inspected his closed fist, opened it and looked at the palm of his hand as though the secrets were all concealed there. He tapped his first finger. 'As I see it, Andrew Keene isn't all he's made out to be. First he put it about that he was made redundant, when really he got the sack.'

'A natural reaction.'

'But it tells us Keene isn't above lying if it suits him.' Stafford tapped a second finger. 'He's at the site when Lindop died.'

'Agreed.'

'Thirdly, from what Forsyth had to say, there could have been a good reason for

123

Keene not liking Lindop too much – the van business.' Stafford inspected his third finger. 'But what's most important of all is the fact that though Keene is supposed to be a bit dreamy, quiet, even gentle, it's on record that not so long ago he used a piece of chain on a driver who was taunting him. And used it to good, bloody effect. So, given the right circumstances, Andrew Keene could get violent. Summing it all up, if I may – Keene was *there,* he had opportunity, he might have had motive, and he could well be the kind of man who is subject to fits of uncontrollable violence.'

Crow sighed. 'You think we should see young Keene as soon as possible.'

'I do.'

'I agree,' John Crow said, and rose to his feet.

CHAPTER IV

1

The dust hung in the late afternoon air, a golden haze that rose lazily until it seemed to touch the intense blue of the sky above Foxholes and edge it with grey-gold cloud. From the top of the hill, where the grass was springy under his feet, Andrew could look down into the quarry and see the stores where he worked, the cutting machines, and the lorries that trundled daily into Northleach. Beyond the quarry were the woods, and the long lifting skyline that stretched into the distance; honey-coloured and grey limestone, dusty roads, grey-walled villages, the golden stubble of fields flanked with clumps of green trees.

Nearer to hand, on the face of the cliff, the men still worked. Andrew's day was over but there were others to whom overtime was the way in which they made a decent living. They clung to the cliff like small dark mice, busying themselves at the quarry. They took out the stone with crowbar and wedge, and then lifted it with pickaxe and shovel, for it was too soft for blasting. It was made up of a myriad shells and tiny fossils and under the thud of dynamite the stone simply crumbled away. Crucial to the beauty of the Cotswolds, essential to preserve the character of Cotswold building, the stone was too expensive to lose so the ancient ways had to do. It was only occasionally that dynamite had to be used, to open up a new area, to cut a new corner – and it had not been used much of recent months.

Andrew sat down on the springy turf and stared back down the hill into the quarry. This was one of the economic realities of life: neither he nor Sara wished to leave the Cotswolds but it was not easy to afford to live there. The coming of the baby made things even more difficult, but what chance did they have? Rich men came out of their retirements from Birmingham and London to drive cottage prices to undreamed of heights. A house selling for four thousand pounds ten years ago would now fetch over thirty thousand on the open market. Sara's nest egg, the legacy of her parents, dwindled in significance when viewed against house prices. Andrew's salary here at the quarry was hardly enough to convince a bank manager he could handle a loan, and a building society manager simply shook his head when asked about the possibility of a mortgage. So what was to be done? The site had been bad enough before – but it had been quiet, at least. Now, there was a constant drift of cars parking, roaring past, creeping along the road outside the site, few of them actually daring to come on to Lovesome Hill Caravan Park but all wanting to see the place where a murder had been committed.

The sun seemed to fade momentarily and Andrew thrust all thoughts of Chuck Lindop from his mind. Somewhere, high above on the wind, a bird was singing. Andrew sat and watched the grey-haired man climbing slowly towards him in the afternoon sunshine.

He was stocky in build, fifty years of age, and he wore his hair in an uncompromising iron-grey stubble. His eyes were bright blue, with the faraway look that a man who lived his life out of doors often held, and his skin was toughened by wind, burned by sun. He had a stolid face and a character to match; not easily moved, he gave an impression of solidity, of strength, of stubborn determination. He was a Cotsaller and as proud of it as all Cotsallers were; he belonged to the 'noicest parrt of England', he claimed he could do almost anything with stone except eat it, and the blackthorn stick he used to help himself up the hill had been fashioned by his own hands. His name was Sam Dixon, and Andrew was waiting for him.

It was possible Sam Dixon sensed it. On other days he would have glanced at

Andrew, nodded and walked on to the bus stop over the rise where the afternoon workers' bus came along at five thirty-five and six-fifteen. He would have stood there, leaning gently on his stick with his knapsack on his back, a little apart from the others, saying little, going his own way. But not today. He came up out of the quarry, saw Andrew seated on the grass and he paused, then stopped. He turned and looked around at the hills about them. He said nothing for several minutes, then slowly he raised his stick, pointed it unwaveringly towards the tiny village nestling against the far slope.

'Them roofs ... loimestone slate, did yer know that? Quite an arrt, puttin' them there. My fayther did them, farty year ago now. That village, he used to tell me, can yer guess how many size of slates there? Near thirty – and each of them 'as a name. Long Bachelors... Short Wivetts...' He shook his head and fell silent again, musing.

'Things were different then,' Andrew said. 'When your father worked about here, I mean.'

Sam Dixon nodded. 'Aye. All good Cotsall stone then. None of this Bradstone mix... They say it *looks* like stone, but oi know it's gravel and cement mixed in moulds and it don't look the same, not to me. Yer can't tell me otherwise.'

'I wouldn't try to.'

Dixon grunted. He glanced back at Andrew, hesitated, then sat down carefully. He gazed around at the distant hills and said, 'You was waitin' for me.'

'That's right. I thought we ought to have a talk.'

'Talk's easy.'

'Sometimes it can help.'

The bright blue eyes looked at him, sharp and belligerent. 'I never saw things that way,' Sam Dixon said. 'Fer me, talk was *niver* the way.'

'Times – and circumstances – change.'

Dixon continued to stare at Andrew, the hostility still bright in his eyes. 'We're talkin' around something, Andrew Keene, and I've no patience for that sort of thing. I like direct talkers, no beatin' about the bush. So what do yer want to say?'

'The dynamite.'

Sam Dixon's eyelids dropped. He turned his head away. When he made no reply, Andrew said, 'It had to be you, Sam.'

'Why do yer say that?'

'I have to keep a book. No explosives go out of the store unless I open up and get a signature for the sticks. We haven't done any blasting for weeks now, and there's no signature in the book. I've been there in the store most of the time and I've signed out – or given out – nothing. But ... well, the police have been around. I had to do a

129

check for the Colonel. Sure enough, there's a couple of sticks missing. The Colonel got excited, wanted to know what happened to them. I couldn't tell him, didn't tell him. The police will be coming back. They'll be questioning every person who had access to the store over the last few months. They'll ask you, Sam.'

'So?'

Andrew's mouth was dry. He swallowed hard. 'Three weeks ago you came into the store – remember? You told me the Colonel wanted me down at the quarry, I had to go at once, you offered to stay and keep shop while I was out. I went to the Colonel – he wanted to speak to me but seemed vaguely surprised I'd come at once. Lunch-hour would have been all right, he said.'

Sam Dixon picked at the turf with his stick. His head was lowered now, his shoulders hunching.

'It had to be then,' Andrew said. 'You lifted a couple of sticks, hid them outside the store, picked them up later.'

'Didn't see me do that.'

'No.'

'Can't be proved, then.' Dixon's sharp eyes glanced at Andrew.

Andrew shook his head. 'No, I can't prove it. Maybe the police will be able to.'

'You're going to tell them, then?'

Andrew shrugged. Dixon eyed him for a

long moment and then dug his stick viciously into the grass. 'Bugger it!'

'It *was* you, Sam, who blew up the generator at the site, wasn't it?' Andrew asked.

'Yer seem to know a bloody lot!'

'No, not know. *Guess.* It's not difficult to guess at the truth when you hear ... rumours.' Andrew hesitated. 'There were rumours, Sam.'

'I don't bloody well doubt it!' Dixon's face became almost savage for a moment, then he looked sideways at Andrew. He shook his head. 'I haven't arsked you how your missus is gettin' on.'

'Pretty good.'

'And the youngster?'

'She'll be in intensive care for another day or so. Trouble with her breathing, but not serious. She should be all right.'

'That's good.' The blue eyes became hazy, clouded with memories. 'Never met your missus, o' course. Saw her with you once though, in Stowford. Fine-lookin' girl. Reminded me of...' He swore suddenly, viciously. 'Aye, I blew that bloody generator! Rumours, you said! Damn it, when it's not rumours, but a worm that crawls in your gut, takes the manhood out of you, addles your brain and makes yer feel madness is aroun' the corner there's nothin' left to do, but to ... blow a generator!' He laughed, but there was a deep bitterness in the sound. 'What a bloody feeble way to try to solve a problem, hey? I could have taken this blackthorn to her, but what would be the good? It was all done, and there was only the gut anger in me, and I just wanted revenge, you know? So there it was – a chance, I took it, grabbed the sticks like you said, and there in the darkness I made a big bang. But what the hell *for?* She's gone, and that was her doin' not his. He'd played his part in the game, but it was her doin' when she left. Took a bloody big slice of my life, she did, not in years maybe, but in...' He waved his hands helplessly, trying to find a word. *Heart* trembled on his lips but he was too angry to admit it, enunciate it, and he discarded it. 'She went off to Oxford and what's left? Just work, and the thought there's no fools like old fools. Forty-five can't marry twenty-five and sleep peaceful. Maybe that's why it went that way in the end. If suspicion's got nothing to feed on, but is still there, maybe the woman suspected feels she's got a right to be hung for a sheep as a lamb.'

'You can't blame yourself, Sam.'

'I didn't! Not then, anyway. No – I blamed that man Lindop! And what did I do about it? *Hah!*'

He struggled to his feet, a stocky angry man with bristling hair and wild blue eyes, a lonely man, an embittered man. He glared at Andrew Keene.

'Ye'll tell them?'

Andrew hesitated, then shook his head. 'No, I'll not tell the police.'

'Why shouldn't you?' Dixon demanded suspiciously.

'It's not my business. It's their problem, not mine.'

'But they'll know the stuff came from your store. How you going to get around *that*?'

Andrew shrugged, making no reply. Sam Dixon stood staring at him, puzzled. They knew each other through the quarry, and not well; Sam Dixon was accustomed to passing the time of day and no more. He was obviously surprised that Andrew Keene should even in the slightest way endanger himself for Sam Dixon, and the surprise bothered him.

'I don't like to be beholden to any man,' Dixon said gruffly.

'You're not beholden. As you've already said, I can't *prove* you took the dynamite or that you blew the generator. I ... I just wanted to find out for my own reasons, and I wanted to warn you that the police will be sniffing around.'

'They–' Dixon hesitated, ran his tongue over dry lips – 'they've no idea yet who ... killed him, then?'

'I wouldn't know.'

'They're not thinking there's a connection between the generator ... and the killing?'

Andrew glanced at Sam Dixon; the man's face was suddenly pale. He shook his head doubtfully. 'I just wouldn't know. But one thing I do know – I'll be saying nothing to them about what you've said.'

Dixon grunted, shifted his weight from one foot to the other. He frowned. 'Aye ... well, I don't understand this, Andrew, but I'm ... grateful. I don't mind standing up for myself, but...'

How could Andrew explain? How could he tell Sam Dixon about the dark horror of that night, explain that he *knew* Dixon had had nothing to do with Lindop's killing?

As Sam Dixon walked away towards the bus stop the police car nosed over the rise and came running gently down towards the quarry. Some twenty yards away from Andrew it slid to a halt. There were two men in the car, apart from the driver. One of them Andrew recognized as the burly detective-inspector who had taken a statement from him the morning after Chuck Lindop had died.

It was the other man who now got out of the car.

He was over six feet tall but stooped slightly. He wore no hat and his head was bald, his forehead domed, his eyes deep-sunken. He was thin, so lean his clothes seemed almost to hang on him, but there was a lightness in his walk that suggested he had been subjected to no illness. Moreover, as he walked towards Andrew he smiled and the smile had a genuine warmth that made one forget the skeletal appearance of the man himself. As he drew closer Andrew could see his eyes too, and detected in them a compassion rare enough to be noticeable.

'My name is Crow – Detective Chief Inspector. You're Andrew Keene, I gather? I thought it might be useful if we had a chat.'

With no more formality than that Crow stretched his tall scarecrow form on the grass beside Andrew, leaning back with his head on his hands, staring at the blue sky. The engine of the police car died as the driver switched off. There was the distant murmur of the workers' bus over the hill and then there was only the bird again, high above them, singing.

'What did you want to talk about?' Andrew asked. His mouth was dry, his heart beginning to thump, but he managed to keep his voice steady enough.

'Oh, various things. You've made your statement. I've read it. There's just a few points I'd like to take up with you.'

'Such as?'

Crow raised his head, smiled as he looked at Andrew as though to suggest there was no such need to hurry. He came up on one elbow.

'Omissions,' he said.

'I don't understand.'

'I'll try to explain. Your statement mentions the following facts: you were at the site all evening; your wife began to have labour pains; you heard the sound of an explosion when the lights went out but did not investigate because you wanted to stay with your wife; you heard no sound of a fight; you stayed with your wife until Ruby Sanders came to the van and heard your wife crying; you ran to the Hartley bungalow and called an ambulance – and that was it?'

Andrew licked his lips. 'Yes, that's about all there was.'

Crow's eyes were sad. 'No omissions?'

'Not that I'm aware of.'

'There are always omissions. People forget. They recall things later. You haven't recalled anything?'

'No.'

Crow sighed. 'Pity. I'd better come clean with you, Andrew. In any investigation arising out of a murder the police have to do all sorts of things – many of them unpleasant. Perhaps the most unpleasant task – at least, I find it unpleasant – is the peeling away we have to do. A man's life is like an onion – peel off one skin, there's another inside. You get told, you learn just so much, until the next layer is exposed. In the middle, somewhere, is the truth – except that the

136

truth is too deep, too personal, ever to be exposed completely.'

'I've told you what I know.'

'That may be so. But there are still things you haven't told us. The explosion at the generator, for instance. There's more than a chance the dynamite came from this quarry – we suspect it did. You've no suspicions in that direction?'

'I can't account for any loss of dynamite,' Andrew said stiffly. 'It's possible some was stolen, of course.'

'You don't know who might have taken some?'

'No,' Andrew lied. Crow watched him carefully in silence for a moment, and Andrew *felt* as though a layer was being stripped away. He began to redden. 'I'd have told you if I'd suspected anything.'

'Would you? Why?'

'Because–' Andrew floundered momentarily – 'because I … I knew Lindop.'

'But you had no reason to like him.'

Andrew went cold. The quick flush that had stained his face faded and he was unable to meet Crow's glance.

'Why do you say that?' he asked.

'This is a *murder* investigation,' Crow said patiently. 'We talk to everyone, and that means relationships between individuals are seen from different angles. One of the people who gave us information was Jack Forsyth.

He told us about the sale of the van to you. He reckons that Chuck Lindop conned you, Andrew. Lindop sold you a van but gave you no proof of ownership, no evidence of the sale. Forsyth told us he asked you for the receipt but you could produce none. Have you found it yet?'

'No.'

'There's the chance Forsyth might argue the van is really his, since it's on his site. But that's between you and him. I'm more interested in what was between you and Lindop.'

Andrew was silent. Crow regarded him contemplatively for a little while and then said, 'There are other things too. You might be able to give me answers, they might be genuine omissions, maybe the officer taking your statement didn't ask the right questions. First of all, there's the chance you might know who Lindop had been dating since he finished with Ruby Sanders.'

Andrew shrugged. 'Several women, I imagine. He was no monk.'

Crow permitted himself a small smile. 'So I gather. But anyone in particular? A married woman, perhaps? There's a rumour he liked married women – no commitment, I suppose.'

Andrew heard the distant murmur of the bus that was taking Sam Dixon back to his lonely house, and he shook his head. 'I don't know of one,' he lied. But he had the odd

138

feeling that Crow sensed the lie, recognized it, *felt* it lying between them, and his heart lurched in his chest.

'All right,' Crow said quietly. 'What about Baker?'

The question was unexpected enough almost to take Andrew's breath away. His startled glance flickered towards Crow, darted away again. 'Baker?' he repeated foolishly.

'You've put it about that you were redundant in your last job. That isn't what your ex-employer says. He gave us two pieces of information: one, you were moody and depressed, not working too well. Second, you attacked Baker, the driver with you in the loading bay, with a piece of chain.'

He waited, and after a long silence Andrew explained. A long, studied provocation that ended with one jibe too many, a sudden surge of uncontrollable violence when the provocation became physical, a piece of chain lying on the ground used part defensively, part offensively.

'I hit him once,' Andrew said. 'I was in a blind rage, but I don't think I really meant to hurt him. Mr Clarke, the manager, I think he knew really what had happened. But he wanted to give me the sack because I hadn't been working too well – living on the site had been ... getting on my nerves. Sara and I hadn't been getting on too well... Anyway,

Clarke gave me the push. I couldn't tell Sara why it had happened. It would have made things … even more difficult between us. So I told her I'd been made redundant. I said I'd not been there long enough for much of a redundancy payment so I had to take the first job I could – the quarry. After that, the story was generally accepted. But you've got to understand, Mr Crow, that piece of violence towards Baker was an isolated thing. I've never on any other occasion–'

'*Never*, Andrew?'

Andrew hesitated. He felt sick and weak; if he'd been standing his legs would have been shaking. It was the same sort of feeling he had experienced once before, one night months ago on the site, when he'd thought his whole world would turn upside down, and the shakiness broke through now in his voice as he said, 'What do you mean?'

Crow studied Andrew's face carefully, as though seeking the truth from his eyes, from the pallor of his skin, the looseness of his mouth. His deep-set eyes were sad.

'The police don't discover the truth from guesswork these days, not often anyway. It's all slog, painstaking questions, moving from one place to another, one person to another, comparing statements, asking more questions… But often enough they are aided by science. The forensic laboratories do wonderful work, Andrew, you wouldn't believe.

140

Let's take the situation where a man has been killed as a result of a struggle. The lab technicians take scrapings of skin, and of nails. They look under the dead man's fingernails, they take fluff from his body. His clothing is subjected to minute analysis. Any stray piece of fibre on the dead man's clothing could match up to fibre found on the man who killed him. Or it could be mud, or hair, or saliva, or blood – and in sexual cases, semen. But you get what I'm driving at, Andrew?'

'No.'

'You mean you don't *want* to. All right, I'll put it more plainly. You have no record of violence, apart from one occasion when you were provoked. Now let's look at Chuck Lindop. It could be argued *he* provoked you too, worried you, caused you anxiety. You would have had reason to go to see him, about the receipt, the day Forsyth called. But Lindop didn't return to the site until nine-thirty or thereabouts. You could have gone to see him at any time after his return. The question is – *did you?* There's nothing about it in your statement. But what will the forensic scientists tell us? We already know there was a struggle in the van. But when the final report comes through will there be evidence that shows us you went there? Fibre, hair, skin? I don't know. Do you? In other words, if you deny you went there, will

141

the laboratory prove you lied?'

Andrew stared at Crow, rigid. His mind was in a turmoil as he thought back unwillingly to the night at the van. He opened his mouth but no sound came. Quietly, Crow said. 'We know there were at least two people there in the van – Lindop and another. Two mugs were used, coffee and probably whisky. It's likely there'll be acceptable prints on the cups. Now think, Andrew, *think!*'

It could be a bluff but he couldn't take the chance. Slowly, Andrew nodded. Crow sat up.

'You went to see Lindop?'

'Yes.'

'What happened?'

'I asked him about the receipt. He got ... offensive. I realized I'd been ... conned. I got angry, took a swing at him, but I missed. He was stronger than me. There wasn't really a fight at all. He turned me around, bundled me out of the van, threw me on to the grass. And then he put on his donkey jacket to go up to look at the generator.'

'There was no fight, more than that?'

'No.'

Crow's eyes seemed to bore into him. In Andrew's mind there was the image of the dead man standing in the doorway scornfully, and his fingers twitched as he felt again the cold iron in his hand as Chuck Lindop turned away, his back to him...

142

'What did you do then, Andrew?'

Andrew Keene dragged himself back to the present, to the sunlight, to the bird singing high above them, to the lies. 'I went back to the van,' he said.

'The last you saw of Lindop he was walking towards the top of the site?'

'Yes.'

'The time?'

'It was… I think it was about ten-fifteen, perhaps a little later, a few minutes maybe. Say five minutes after the generator was blown up. Not more than that.'

'And you stayed with your wife then, until the ambulance came?' Crow asked.

'She was crying, moaning. She was getting these pains. I stayed with her till Ruby came and then I went to the Hartley place to phone the ambulance.'

Crow was silent for a while. At last he rose, brushing loose grass from his jacket and trousers. Andrew rose also; he was about the same height as Crow, but slim where Crow was skinny. Maybe when he was older he would be like the policeman. In some ways.

'How is your wife?' Crow asked.

'She's recovering well. The … the birth was a bit of a shock to her. Bad labour – an operation. But two weeks and she'll be … they'll both be all right.'

'She … she'll be able to corroborate what you've told me?'

'She'll know I went up to the van. The fight … I haven't talked to her about it.'

'Mmm.' Crow hesitated. 'You know, Andrew, I'll have to follow this up with the laboratory people. But I'm glad you told me. It's better you telling than me finding out. And I *would* have found out.' He paused again, watching Andrew carefully. Andrew swallowed, injected innocence into his eyes, sincerity into his tone.

'*I didn't kill Chuck Lindop*,' he said.

Crow nodded, slowly, then turned away. The burly detective-inspector had got out of the squad car and was standing with one hand raised. As Crow drew near him Andrew heard the man's words.

'There's a radio call – I think you ought to take it. Could be we're getting closer already.'

2

The aspect of the Cotswolds that never failed to fascinate John Crow was the strange contrasts the area offered. He could stand in a broad street in which the rattle of the mail-coaches still seemed to echo on a quiet Sunday afternoon and see in the clear sky above the vapour trail of a supersonic aircraft. It was the paradox of the Cotswolds – the Middle Ages and the Jet Age lay in

144

close proximity. Ancient churches and mellowed stone, the Red Arrows trailing plumes of coloured smoke above Little Rissington, a nine-hundred-year-old hotel at Kingham offering a 'small helicopter pad' for the use of its guests, memorial brasses to the old wool merchants and jaded business-men tasting the calm of the morning with the local hunt – it was all part of the life of the Cotswolds and yet there were times when the contrasts could jar.

This was one of them.

The town boasted a stream which had fed the mill to dye and shrink and thicken the cloth; the local pub was called the Fleece; small handicrafts shops sprouted in the main street and the nave of the church had recently been redone in Bradstone slates. But the hotel on the edge of the town was long, low, modern and ugly. It was fringed with drooping trees that had never accepted their transplanting with a glad heart, and fronted by a pink gravel car park that clashed noisily with the yellow 'reconstructed' stone of the external walls of the hotel. To see it was to ask how it had ever got past a plan-ning committee; to ask the question was to guess that there were undeclared interests on the committee. It was sad and annoying, but not new. But it put Crow in an evil mood. He had been too close to the Cotswolds as a boy to be able to suffer desecration gladly.

He strode across the car park with Inspector Stafford just behind him; his head was low, jutting forward, and his stride lengthened with the depth of his annoyance. It was still with him as he put out a hand one second before the electronically operated glass doors whispered away from him and he stamped into the foyer in a thoroughly bad humour.

The manager had long, carefully-dressed fair hair and a blue suit, white patterned shirt and gold tie. He was young, and nervous. He came forward displaying a length of carefully laundered cuff and gold cufflinks.

'My name is Daly.'

'Crow.' Disinclined in his present humour to indulge in formalities, Crow added, 'Now what's this all about?'

'I explained over the phone.'

'Explain again. And at more length.' As Daly was about to speak Crow held up his hand. 'But not here. Your office, perhaps?'

Daly led the way quickly, threading past the gleaming counter and the potted plants, into the office beyond. He ushered out a girl working on some accounts, gestured Crow and Stafford to chairs and perched himself on the edge of his desk. 'Well,' he began, 'when this woman turned up and asked–'

'No,' Crow interrupted. 'From the beginning, please.'

It was quickly enough told. Daly had been

appointed manager of the hotel a year previously. Shortly after he had arrived he had taken to spending the odd evening in the hotel lounge 'to get to know the clientele' and one evening had struck up an acquaintance with one of the customers who had a request which was unusual in one respect. While residents at the hotel often enough made use of the hotel safe deposit system for their valuables they always removed these valuables when they left. This request was different in that the applicant was not a resident, though he wanted to use the deposit for a while.

'I saw nothing wrong in the matter,' Daly explained. 'After all, if we needed the deposit box there was no problem – we could merely tell him we couldn't keep his papers for him any longer. And if he was prepared to trust us while he was not a resident, well, in a way that was rather flattering, don't you think? He explained, of course, that he didn't want to use a bank because they weren't the *safest* of places – he said accountants sometimes insisted on knowing what you had in the bank before they'd make up your accounts. Well, I don't know about that – indeed, I didn't want to know about it. As far as I was concerned, since he was prepared to pay for the convenience, that was all right by me.'

The arrangement had been made. The hotel kept some twenty small deposit boxes in which guests' valuables could be placed. A key was handed to the guest, a duplicate key held by the hotel staff. Both keys had to be used to open the boxes.

'So he paid for his key, I brought out the box, he put his stuff in it – bonds, he told me, and insurance policies – he locked it, I locked it, and into the big safe it went with the others. And that was that, really. He came in from time to time, had a drink, never went near his box, but that wasn't my affair. He paid up three months in advance so that was okay. And then it happened.'

He had been off duty, he explained. He had spent the day in London with some friends and hadn't seen the newspaper at all until he was actually travelling back by train. Idly, he had picked up the evening paper someone had left on the seat; thumbing through it he came across the report of a murder.

'Well, I mean, the name leapt out at me! After all, it isn't *every* day you see that someone you know has been given the chop, if I can put it like that! Of *course*, I was *intrigued*. As soon as I got back to the hotel I thought of that deposit box and I went along there, but I found that it was no longer in use. I questioned the staff, and it finally came out that the desk clerk – Frances, she's called, a nice kid – recalled a man coming in the previous day with the key. He'd asked for the box, she'd provided our key when he showed his and gave his name. He emptied the box, left his key, went off. That was that.'

Of course, he hadn't really known what to do. If this 'smart, dark man' that Frances had described had come along to empty the box that was one thing; the fact he'd come to the hotel the morning after the depositor was dead was another.

'But what was I to do? I mean, what would you have done in my place? Gone to the police? Not at all. Look at it from my point of view. In the first place, this small dark man could have been given the key quite legitimately before the owner was killed. Secondly, he could have been the real owner – maybe he'd been acting previously through an agent. It *does* happen. But if I'm to be perfectly honest, and I'm trying to be, believe me, there was another important consideration in my mind. Trouble. This *is* my first managerial post, after all. It's true there was nothing wrong in renting out the deposit box to a non-resident but it was certainly ... *irregular*. It's a point that would clearly have been raised by my employers. And finally, what harm had been done? How would it help matters if I came running to the local police with stories of Mr Lindop having had a deposit box here but it was now empty? I mean, there's an awful lot of small dark men running around

149

in England. And, well, yes, I agree, I was being defensive. After all, if the name of a *murdered* person gets linked in any way with the hotel, it does something to the clientele, doesn't it?'

One could never tell what it would do, there was the chance it could increase the popularity of the hotel, but popularity by itself was not necessarily what an hotel would want. There was always the question of the *class* of person who would be attracted to an hotel, and there was the danger that if people came to think that the sort of person who got himself murdered frequented the hotel, they might be disinclined to patronize it further. One visit, out of curiosity perhaps, and then the goodbye kiss.

'So I said nothing. Until today. And it's not a *long* silence, is it? I mean, nothing much can have happened in the couple of days I've said nothing. No fleeing from the country or anything like that. But the thing is, my hand was forced. I mean, I immediately saw where my duty lies the moment this woman came into the hotel and began making enquiries about the deposit box. It's just fortunate that there was that squad car down at the junction – I could see it from my office window – so I could send one of the waiters to fetch them quickly, while I detained the woman in the foyer. And after that, well, here *you* are. The woman I mentioned? Oh, she's in room nineteen. I've had tea served to her, and sandwiches, while she waited there for you. I mean, we have to maintain the reputation of the hotel for *service*. You just never know, do you...?'

The woman was about thirty-five years old. Her hair was the colour of tin and she was teasing strands of it with fingers that trembled on the edge of nervousness without quite going over – yet. She was well-built and her dress was just that little bit tight enough to suggest she might be open to offers. Her face had the puffiness of discontent, the flesh swollen by the blows that fate and drink had dealt her; her eyes were intelligent, but vulnerable, suggesting she deserved better of this life. She looked at Crow as he entered the room and he caught a brief flash of all the defeats and the disillusionments and despairs that had come her way, badly, cruelly, undeservedly. But the flash was gone in a moment, her eyes were masked, and the other shields came up, the protection that enabled her to make her woman's way in a man's world.

The manager, Daly, twitched at his gold tie, exposed an inch of shirtcuff. She gestured to the tea beside her elbow, untouched. 'Thanks. Right colour. Wrong taste. But thanks, anyway.' Daly seemed pleased. He nodded, gave a slightly nervous giggle and introduced John Crow.

The woman sat heavily in her chair, indifference scarring her glance. But there was a defensiveness about her too; she was wary and ready to expose claws that she was not averse to unsheathing.

'I'm sorry you've been kept waiting like this,' Crow said smoothly. 'And if the officers who ... detained you here like this were ... insistent, once again, I'm apologetic. It simply seemed easier ... it was easier for me and my colleagues to get here rather than have you escorted to Stowford where we have our headquarters.'

He introduced George Stafford, then waited. The woman made no reply. 'Would you mind telling us who you are?' Crow asked at last.

She hesitated, thought it over for a moment, then almost swallowed the words.

'Honey Lindop,' she said, and glanced involuntarily at the ring on her finger.

Casually, Crow half turned and reached for an upright chair. He caught Stafford's glance; the inspector was pursing his lips in a silent whistle of surprise but Crow's features were expressionless. He sat down and Stafford stepped back to lean against the wall behind him.

'Mrs Lindop... I take it that you are related to the recently deceased Chuck Lindop?'

'Charles.' She almost snarled the word. 'I

always called him Charles because he hated his real name. *Chuck.*' Her voice was harsh but not uncultivated; she had worked at her accent over the years and even dissatisfaction could not destroy training.

'Perhaps you would like to tell me what you are doing here?'

The fingers that still teased at her tin-coloured hair belied the casual tone she employed. 'Easy. When my husband Charles Lindop died I thought it was about time that he made some contribution to the life style I've been indulging in – or would have indulged in if he'd ever kept to his promise to send me the money.'

'What money?'

'Maintenance.' She almost jeered as she said it. 'Me and Charles, we were married seven years. After three I found out he was playing the field as though he was still a young buck among the does. We had a few quarrels, and then he went his way, I went mine. But he promised me maintenance. When I made things a bit hot for him from time to time he paid me a little. But usually, it just wasn't worth the effort. So most times I left him alone. I had my job – I work for an estate agent – so I could manage.'

'No divorce?'

'What for?' Something happened to her eyes, as though old, worn cinema films were flickering through her mind, faded images of something that had once been, and the hope of something that could yet be again. 'He didn't want it – it's useful having a wife in name if you get too tangled with another urgent female – and me, I was indifferent.' She grinned suddenly, unexpectedly, and it changed her face, gave it a light and a glow that removed years of disgust from her features. 'Or maybe I really thought he'd come back some time. Stupid, hey? I mean, he was a *real* bastard. But then women like me behave irrationally over men like Charles Lindop. In the beginning, we see only the charm. Later, we're hooked, and it's like a drug. Later still, when everything blows up in our faces, we still think it's all a bad dream, and in the end, bad dreams are just that – bad dreams. And the reality is something you just live with. But always with a flicker of hope. Just a flicker.'

'And what was the reality with you, Mrs Lindop?'

She picked up the dark glasses that lay beside the cold tea. 'Acceptance. I knew eventually that I couldn't take him any more. So we split. And I didn't really expect him to come back. Afterwards, I didn't really want him to. I had my job at Northleach – I could make my own way – but when I heard he'd … well, I thought he might well have left some cash lying around and it seemed right I should have first claim–'

'Did you try his bank?'

Honey Lindop laughed. It was a bizarre sound, half way between contempt and annoyance and untouched by humour.

'Bank! Chuck would have *robbed* one rather than put cash into one. No, I wasn't surprised to learn he'd put his money here. It was the kind of nutty thing he'd do, believe me.'

'How *did* you know he'd made a deposit here?'

She was silent for a moment, her calculating eyes fixed on Crow. She toyed with her glasses, clicking them against the teacup. She shrugged.

'You can check, I suppose. I've been to thirteen hotels today and yesterday. They say thirteen is unlucky, well, the fourteenth was unlucky for me. This one. Because I find the place all right but, the money's gone. How did I know about it? Chuck did it before. Safe as houses, he used to laugh, hotels. I knew there'd be no bank account. But I didn't know which hotel. So it meant travelling. And I was too late.'

'Someone else lifted the money?' Crow said.

'Exactly.'

'How much was there?'

'I didn't say–' she began, and then paused, thinking.

Crow waited and Honey Lindop pulled

herself upright in her chair. She looked around the room listlessly as though seeking some place to hide and cry. She shrugged.

'Haven't a clue. If there was anything.'

'You said you came looking for money.'

'I didn't say there was any there,' she countered. 'Last time I saw Chuck he was pretty slewed, he told me he had a nest egg–' involuntarily her glance slipped around the room as though she suspected it might yet be in there – 'but that's not the same thing as saying he had any cash hidden away here. Anyway, even if he had, what's the odds? Somebody else's lifted it.'

'Who?'

'You tell me.' For a moment a fierce anger burned in her eyes. 'Tell me and I'll put my nails in him.'

A moment, and she was in control again. She stared at the floor trying not to be aware of Crow's glance. When she was asked if she had anything to add she shook her head without speaking. Crow soon found the way to open the floodgate, however. 'You described your … husband as a real bastard, Mrs Lindop. I'd be grateful if you'd fill in the picture a little more fully. We don't know a great deal about him.'

She did it with relish. In the background, George Stafford's pencil flew over his note book as Honey Lindop's malicious voice tore into the character that had been Charles

Lindop. He had been a useless, whoring, puffed-up pimp, good in bed and bad at everything else. He couldn't keep his hands off other people's money or other men's women. He was unreliable and untrustworthy, he'd take every last penny from your purse and every stitch of clothes off your back. He made friends easily and enemies even more easily and lots of his friends were soon enemies. In a party he was great; in private he was a swine. He could con you with a smile in his voice, and stamp on your face when your back was turned. 'And that,' she added drily, 'takes some doing, I don't need to tell you.'

'But you didn't hate him, Mrs Lindop.'

Honey started as if she had been slapped. Her eyes slid a glance around the room as though seeking escape from the question. She circled her lips with a pale, nervous tongue. 'No,' she said. 'I didn't hate him.'

'You remained on reasonably good terms with him.'

'I had to live.'

'I gather he had a certain charm,' Crow said drily. 'I'm told he was popular with women. He could–'

'*Use* you,' Honey Lindop said bitterly. The interruption seemed to spark off some flash of nervous energy in her; she came to life like a rumbling volcano, letting off sparks and steam and pain. 'For God's sake. Why

157

do I dredge around in my mind for excuses for him! He doesn't need them now, not that he ever did. He was a bastard, and he died a bastard. He conned me, he conned his friends, he conned everyone he met, but he was such a *small* man! You know that story about inside every fat man there's a thin one tryin' to get out? That's how it was with Chuck Lindop – he was a *small* man, with a *big* one trying to get out from inside. But the trouble was he never *would* be big. He had ideas, did Charles Lindop! He thought he was smart, and clever, a genius; he thought he could handle people, make them sing his tune and never get off-key. He thought he could manipulate people and there'd never be a come-back. He was so bloody *clever*, and one day, he knew, he'd really make it. A big one, the big time, the day it would all go right for him and he'd have a Rolls, a country house, and money in the bank. But it was all a dream. While he saw himself as Mr Big inside, other people saw him for what he was, a small con-man, picking up small cash in small ways. Tough, but not tough enough. Dirty, and ready to do the dirt, but not big enough to lay it on really thick where there could be a real pay-off. He had one real talent for women. He could charm all sorts of birds out of all sorts of nests, but beyond that he was nothing. Just small. *Small.*'

There was a fine film of spittle on her lips. She wiped it off, surprised, perhaps at the wetness of her mouth, perhaps at the uncontrolled vehemence of her tongue. With the surprise came something else – a hint of fear. Something was going on at the back of her eyes and she seemed shaken by her own vehemence. As Crow stared at her he could almost sense the fumbling that was going on in her mind, the check she was making of words and phrases she had used, testing them, trying them out again, looking for something, searching. But the anxiety was dying as she calmed, returned Crow's gaze.

'One thing's for sure,' she said, more quietly. 'I don't have the first idea who killed him.'

'Or why he was killed?' Stafford asked from behind Crow.

Honey Lindop shook her head. 'Not that either. But if you want my guess, *cherchez la femme*. Charles Lindop needed women like other men need air. There'll be a slap and tickle in it somewhere. I'm telling you.'

'You know Ruby Sanders?' Crow asked.

Honey Lindop showed her teeth. The grimace passed for a smile. She nodded. 'Ruby took over there for a while. Bouncy little tart. Chuck moved her down the field. There's been others since then, though. The latest ... well, I did hear a rumour and saw him with a woman some time ago. Married to someone working at the quarry, I believe. You check it out and I reckon you'll find there's a jealous husband in it somewhere.'

3

John Crow spent the next morning at the forensic laboratories. The pathologist in charge was eager and determined to show all his wares. Crow allowed himself to be shown the lines of test tubes bearing the hairs, the fibres, the materials and the body fluff, the slides with blood specimens, the photographs of the murder weapon, the shots of the deceased; the list seemed endless. It was late morning before he was able to pin the pathologist down to answer the questions he wanted to ask. And then they were vague enough.

'First, the cause of death. Pretty clear. The crowbar was almost certainly the weapon, the haemorrhage the cause of death. A thinnish skull, splintering; the blow not too heavy, but direct. A right-handed person, standing just behind the deceased as he faced forward. Medium height – maybe five-seven, five-nine.'

'The struggle he had been involved in?'

'I would say brief, and not very significant to the death itself. There are traces which might lead to an identification but evidentially, as you'll appreciate, they would not necessarily correlate. I mean, we might show that Mr A struggled with the deceased; we could not show the deceased died as a result of the struggle. It could show motivation of course. And all this presupposes you can find Mr A. A for Attacker, you see?'

'Time of death?'

'Ahhh. I so fear that question. So many policemen regard it as a crucial factor, but no sensible doctor would dare go into the witness box and state the exact time of death merely from deductions arising out of a post-mortem change in the body. You will have non-medical evidence which gives a lead?'

'Lindop was alive at ten-fifteen. He was dead at eleven.'

'Ahhh. I think we can be more precise than that. As you may know, the rate of loss of heat from a cadaver offers a reliable method of estimating the time which has elapsed since death, up to about twenty-four hours. But it means a careful study of the cooling curve – it has a sigmoid form, you know – after collection of the relevant data: air temperature reading, rectal reading, determination of the constants. Now, in the case of the deceased, taking him as average to fat in build, we could suggest a regular decrease of one point five degrees Fahrenheit per hour. The body was clothed, so adjustments are necessary but–'

'Time of death?'

'Don't quote me in court but I'd say after ten-fifteen, before ten-thirty. Press me and I'd say ten-twenty. Ask me to enter the regions of fantasy and hypothesis and I'd say ten twenty-three. But I'd never be able to prove it. Near enough for your purposes, Chief Inspector Crow?'

'Near enough,' George Stafford grunted, 'but where does it get us?'

'Not very far,' Crow said gloomily. He stood by the window with his hands in his pockets, staring out over Stowford Broadway. The fair was over, the gipsies were packing up and leaving. Already the ranks of painted caravans showed gaps and one ancient vehicle was trundling away with an impatient lorry on its tail. The swarthy gipsy holding the reins ignored the lorry horn with an assurance born of indifferent superiority. He was small and dark. He could have been the man who emptied Lindop's deposit box. So could fifty other people in Stowford alone. Crow shook his head. 'Not very far,' he repeated.

He turned away and Stafford looked up expectantly. 'At least the street will be quieter,' Crow said with irritation in his voice.

'And maybe we'll get no more calls about

Northleach Hall.'

'You've had another?'

Stafford nodded. 'Yesterday. The caller refused to give his name again, but said that Northleach Hall was going to be done. Well, we don't get too much of that kind of robbery around here, so maybe now the gippoes are off it'll all come to nothing. The Chief Constable has ordered a watch on the Hall anyway – he hunts from time to time with the owner.'

'Our hunt's of a different kind,' Crow said sourly. 'But let's look at what we have so far. If we assume the pathologist is right about the timing of the death – and we have to assume that – the pattern of events seems to be like this… Lindop arrived back at the site about nine-thirty. Keene visited him at about ten o'clock. By ten-fifteen they had quarrelled and Lindop threw Keene out of the van. He then returned to his wife, who was beginning to have labour pains.'

'Right. According to Ruby Sanders's statement, she drew up in the lane outside the camp at about ten-fifteen or ten-twenty. She had a minor struggle with her octopus salesman – incidentally, we've managed to trace him now and he should be through here by tomorrow morning to make a statement – and then she went on the site at approximately ten forty-five.'

'Keene phoned at eleven o'clock, the

163

ambulance arrived, the body was found, the police got to the site at eleven-fifty and the residents began drifting back from Stowford Fair, Samson being one of the first, just before midnight. Those are the only ones who would seem to be pretty positive about their timings. Now then, the explosion...'

Stafford consulted the notes in front of him. 'Everyone seems to agree that this occurred at about ten-ten. Hartley, Keene, Mrs Keene, the people up the road by the bus stop. It would seem to be right – the culprit must have left the lane before Ruby Sanders arrived.'

'And the culprit–?'

Stafford scratched his nose reflectively. 'From the remarks passed by Mrs Lindop, and the rumours we've checked out on, it would seem it could have been a quarryman called Sam Dixon. His wife left him recently: she's twenty years younger than him and had certainly been seen in Lindop's company. He *could* have lifted some dynamite from Keene's stores, and he *could* have blown the generator out of spite, getting his own back on Lindop. But whether he also thumped Lindop on the back of the head, in the darkness...'

'There's enough people with *motive*,' Crow said. 'This man Dixon, angry because Lindop seduced his wife; Forsyth maybe, angry because he was being swindled; Ruby

164

Sanders, possibly, if she never really got over being dropped by Lindop—'

'And Andrew Keene.'

'Yes … Andrew Keene. He must still be a front runner,' Crow admitted reluctantly. 'I hardly think it likely he would kill Lindop simply because he felt he'd been cheated, but he *is* capable of sudden violence, he does admit to fighting with Lindop, and he was the only other person on the site—'

'But that still doesn't explain the deposit box, and just where Honey Lindop fits in.'

'It doesn't, indeed. I seemed to detect something odd in the relationship between Mrs Lindop and her husband. Did you notice anything?'

Stafford shrugged. 'Not in particular. She seems to me to have come to a compromise about the man. She saw his faults – recognized them – and in the end she just didn't care. Except for the money.' He paused. 'She's been making her own way in her job.'

'At the estate agents?'

'Yes. I checked. She goes down well when the men take a look at houses; she has a good line, I gather. And she's got herself interested in the valuation line too. Learns quickly apparently. A small firm, and she's proved useful.'

'I just find it odd,' Crow said. 'If she was making her own way, and separated from Lindop, why did she maintain contact with him? Oh, I know she hasn't *said* as much, but they were still on reasonably good terms and I just wonder if their contact was more regular than she'd have us believe.'

'You mean they slept together occasionally?'

'No, not that.' Crow shook his head, frowning. 'I'll have to think about it. Just vague notions. And that deposit box … it bothers me…' In sudden decision Crow headed for the door. 'I'm going out to the camp again. I think you ought to take a closer look at that Dixon fellow; I'll have another chat with Ruby Sanders. She knew Lindop for a while, stayed in his van and his bed. Maybe he talked to her about a deposit box; if he did, he might also have talked to her about Honey Lindop…'

It was a grey afternoon. Dark clouds lay banked against the hills and there was a fine rain mist in the distance, not enough to make the roads wet but forming a damp pattern on the windscreen of the car. Crow had dispensed with a driver: the Chief Constable was already champing over the manpower demands Crow had made – he had traffic to control, after all. So, while others did the grinding work of comparing statements and making the usual checks, Crow made his own contribution to the Chief Constable's peace of mind by driving himself. Besides, he liked to be alone in countryside like this.

Not that it was the best of days to enjoy the Cotswolds. The mist obscured much of the distant hills, and in a short while he was in the lane outside the site anyway, walking its length, noting distances, checking the place where Ruby had parked with her salesman Romeo, observing the bungalow from which Keene had made his telephone call that night. Hartley. Crow hadn't interviewed him yet. There'd be time to repair that omission later.

Crow drove on to the site.

He noted a twitch of the curtains at the Sharkey van, and Mrs Williams peered from her window as he got out of the car. He ignored them. They'd given statements, and there was nothing to suggest they had been implicated in any way in the fiddles or amours or death of Chuck Lindop. The Keene van seemed to be empty, though the door was ajar. Crow walked to Ruby Sanders's van but there was no one inside. He turned around, stared across the site – and then he saw them.

The woods were perhaps twenty yards wide at their narrowest point, forty at their broadest. They ran along the length of the site, effectively screening it from the main road beyond. The trees themselves were sorry enough – scrub alder, rowan, a scattering of silver birch, bent away from the prevailing wind and tangled with under-growth, nettles, tins and broken bottles. They were certainly not thick enough to effectively screen the couple at work among them. Crow walked slowly across the site, over the gravel path and up to the edge of the trees. Andrew Keene was straightening, leaning on a shovel. He put a hand out, touched Ruby Sanders on the shoulder as he saw John Crow. Ruby started, turned, and looked towards Crow.

She was crying.

The bounce and the confidence seemed to have deserted her. She seemed smaller, her lacquered hair had succumbed to her grief, and her nose was red, her eyes swollen with weeping. She made no attempt to control it; she sobbed as she scrambled through the undergrowth with Andrew just behind her, and as she drew near Crow heard her say one word.

'Patch.'

She could take the end of an affair with a careless shake of her hip; she could endure snide remarks and come back with a few of her own; she could be used and conned, and grin at her own foolishness; but she couldn't take the loss of her dog.

'What happened?' Crow asked.

She shook her head and pushed her way past him, to run all the way to her van. The sexuality was gone from her; she looked small, and pathetic, and suddenly middle-aged. Crow turned and looked at Andrew Keene. The young man stood diffidently holding the shovel. He seemed unable, or unwilling, to meet Crow's glance.

'You've just buried the dog?' Crow asked quietly.

Keene nodded, saying nothing.

'How did it die?'

Keene raised his head, stared around the site with a frown on his face. He thudded the shovel against the turf impatiently, and shrugged. 'Run down by a car.'

'Here? On the site?'

Keene looked at Crow angrily, as though asking whether it really mattered now that the dog was dead. He had been fond of the animal, Crow guessed, and he was upset also at Ruby's distress. He shook his head.

'On the road, I think. Ruby came over this morning, after I returned from the hospital, told me Patch had been run over, and she'd collected him. Herself. She had him in a wooden box. I just carried the box and buried it. Ruby's very upset. I didn't question her too much about it. I'd better go down to see her. She'll need a drink, I reckon.'

'Do you think–' Crow began, then stopped. This was no time to ask Ruby questions, and Keene's eyes told him so. He was a little surprised at the determination in the young man's eyes, and also at the posi-

169

tive way in which he strode down towards Ruby's caravan. He had not thought of Andrew Keene as a man a woman could rely on, but given the right circumstances perhaps Andrew could be strong... There could be steel in the dreamer. In an odd way the thought did not comfort Crow. Andrew Keene was not Crow's idea of a killer, but if there really was steel in him...

Carefully, Crow walked into the woods. He found the mongrel's grave easily enough. He stood near the freshly turned earth and stared at it thoughtfully. Dogs died every day and people mourned them. And they died in different ways. More than a few got knocked down by cars. But Patch knew his way around. He had lived on the site for several years with his mistress. That wouldn't prevent him getting knocked down on the main road, but there were accidents ... and accidents.

Indecisively, Crow walked back through the trees and looked down towards Ruby's van. It was ridiculous, really, a policeman holding back from questioning someone because a scruffy little mongrel had died. But a man couldn't help the way he was made, and if there were traits in John Crow that made him less efficient as a policeman but more human as a person, well, that was no bad thing. Besides, his journey would not be wasted – he could always go to see the man in the bungalow. Hartley.

Crow left his car where it was and walked up through the site. The rain had drifted lower now and he could feel its damp hand on his bald head. He walked out into the lane, turned in at the bungalow gate where Andrew Keene would have run that night to phone for the ambulance for Sara, and rang the bell at the front door. There was a shuffling sound inside, after an interval, and Crow saw the figure of a man behind the glass panel of the door. A lock clicked, the door opened, and the two men stared at each other in surprise.

John Crow was the first to recover. His journey certainly had not been wasted. He grinned, in a wicked delight.

'Well, hello, *Fred!* I didn't know you were Mr Hartley! Can I come in?'

CHAPTER V

1

It rained heavily during the night and John Crow woke twice to the violent drumming of rain against his window. When he looked out at seven in the morning it was to a pale sun, and the Broadway looked as though it had been swept clean. There were no gipsy caravans, the street itself gleamed wetly in the sunshine and the woodland on the hill beyond was dark, bright green. Crow breakfasted well – kidneys and bacon crisped as beautifully as Martha could ever do – and drank three cups of coffee before he made his way across to the operations room at Stowford Police Station. There was every sign that the sun would continue to shine all day – it was to be no early morning brightness followed by dark clouds of rain – and it gave a corresponding lift to his spirits. He wished the startled constable inside the door a hearty good morning and made his way to his office. He sat down with his files and began to go through them painstakingly. When George Stafford arrived some twenty minutes later he nodded to him, then went on reading. Stafford went out, and came back in a half hour later.

'That salesman we've been looking for has arrived. And did you send a squad car for Mr Hartley?'

'I did. But he can wait. Will you ask a constable to cheer him up with a cup of coffee? I've no doubt he's wearing his best hangdog expression.'

Stafford grinned. 'He isn't looking too happy, that's for sure. I gather you know him?'

'Of old,' Crow said grimly. 'But we'll come to that. First of all, settle him down. Then I'd be grateful if you could let me have the file on that recent burglary you told me about–'

'Cobham Park? Well, that's hardly *recent*–'

'That, and anything you have on the tip-offs about Northleach Hall being given the once-over. There *has* been an informer, hasn't there?'

Stafford nodded, obviously somewhat puzzled as to why Crow should be interested in mere burglaries when he should be more concerned about the murder investigation he was conducting. 'Do you think I need to tell Inspector Edwards you're looking at the files? He's in charge of the cases.'

'Not necessary. I just want some inform-ation, that's all. But if he does ask, tell him I might have something for him later. That'll cheer him up, no doubt.'

Stafford went out, and a few minutes later a chubby constable came in with a file which he handed to John Crow. It contained several papers, a number of statements, and it made fairly interesting reading.

Cobham Park was a fifteenth-century mansion house set in about twelve acres of ground. It was owned by a retired major who used it as a summer retreat and a place where he could entertain friends. It contained a number of not very valuable paintings, and a certain number of rather more valuable items of jewellery which for some curious reason the major had thought would be more safe in the vault in the house than in London. There was an inventory of the baubles in the file – about a year previously they had been valued by a local agency with a view to sale when the major had lost rather a lot on a grey mare called Chester Lady – and the total value came to a little over twenty-five thousand pounds.

The burglary had taken place eight months ago. It had been a botched, bungled job. They had been lucky with the alarm system – it was inefficient and rang only when the police entered. The burglars had smashed in a door panel, broken three windows and generally rampaged through the house when they found themselves unable to break into the vault where the valuables were kept. No fingerprints had been left – at least they had taken the precaution of wearing gloves, but in every other way the break-in showed signs of having been an amateur affair. It had all been very crude, unprofessional – and a waste of time. No arrests had been made, and after the attempt to steal the jewels they had been removed by the major to London.

'Not before time,' Crow murmured to himself.

A brief note, a carbon copy from another file, was appended, dealing with Northleach Hall. A call had been made from a public telephone box six weeks ago; the caller refused to give his name but said that 'the police might be interested to know that Northleach Hall had been cased, and a job was likely in the near future.' The second call had come after an interval of a month. It gave no new information, but simply reiterated the previous information. The Stowford police had followed the matter up, kept a watch on the premises and had warned the owner. He was a local magistrate who had bought the Hall some nine months previously, found his wife didn't like its draughty corridors, and was putting it up for sale again. To date, although the property was in the hands of several agents, no offers had been made. When Crow saw the price being asked he wasn't surprised.

The only other note on the file recorded

that the two calls from the phone box had not been traced to any known informer. They could have been a hoax, but in view of the burglary at Cobham Park it was as well to be safe.

As Crow finished reading the file there was a tap on the door and Stafford returned. He held the door wide. 'Mr James Glanville,' he announced.

The man who entered was big across the shoulders but bigger around the stomach. He had wavy hair of a uniform blackness that suggested it owed not a little to art. His eyes were bright, his nose strong, his mouth weak, his chin cleanly shaven and deeply indented. He was smiling a smile of utter insincerity; it had edges of nervousness and suggested he really wanted to be liked but there were occasions, incredibly, when he was not.

'Did you drive up this morning?' Crow asked.

'I did. But no harm. I was on my way to Cheltenham anyway, and Stowford isn't too far out of my way. Besides, anything to help.'

Crow waved him to a seat, and asked him if he would like some coffee. Glanville replied affirmatively so Stafford went out and arranged for three cups to be brought in. They talked in desultory fashion about the route Glanville had taken up to Stowford until the coffee arrived and then Crow came to the point.

'You'll have been told by the local police that we're making enquiries into the death of Charles Lindop at Lovesome Hill Caravan Park.'

'That's right.' Glanville took a hasty sip of coffee and managed to hide his distaste with a rapid smile that came and went like sunlight on a shadowed hill. 'Not that there's much I can tell you.'

'We appreciate your coming along to talk to us. I imagine it could be somewhat ... embarrassing for a man in your position.'

Glanville glanced at Crow, then at Stafford. He took a quick decision, was prepared to regard them both as men of the world. 'I've got a wife – who understands me only too well. But I believe the police can be souls of discretion in these situations. So, that's the way I'd like it. She doesn't know I'm coming here to ... help in enquiries.'

'There's no need she should,' Crow murmured. 'Now then ... you went to Lovesome Hill that night you were in the area?'

'That's right.' Glanville hesitated. 'But I didn't go on the site at all. Just parked in the lane for a while, then set out on the drive home. My wife was surprised to see me, but not displeased. I'd told her I wouldn't be back that night, but in the circumstances there seemed to be no point in hanging around Stowford any longer. So I went home. Got in about three in the morning.'

'I think it would be best if you started from the beginning,' Crow suggested. 'You were with a woman called Ruby Sanders…'

Glanville tightened his stomach muscles, pulled his stomach in as though expecting her to walk into the room. He nodded. 'That's it. I'd finished my business at four so drove down to Stowford. I thought with the fair on there'd be … something going, you know what I mean. As it happened, I hung around after a meal and saw nothing worthwhile, you know, and was regarding it as a wasted evening when Ruby walked in.'

'You'd met her before?'

'Hell, no!' Glanville looked indignant at the thought he should ever meet the same woman twice on a night out. 'I was getting a drink at the bar, it was crowded, she came up behind me, fumbled in her purse and asked me if I could catch the barman's eye for her, but I knew she was really trying to catch mine. I didn't mind; she's a bouncy little bit, and I got her a drink, refused her money and took her company instead. This was in that pub across the way. We had a few drinks there, got chatting, she was happy enough and quite prepared for a bit of nuzzling in the pub, so I knew I was on to a good thing.' A puzzled frown touched his brow. 'At least, I thought I was on to a good thing.'

'What happened?'

'Well, that was it. Nothing.'

'You took her out to your car?'

'Yes, sure. She told me she had a van out at the caravan site and she directed me. We pulled into the lane and she told me to stop. She said she didn't want to go on the site because the neighbours might talk – though I'd have thought they would have had plenty to talk about before then. No sweat, I didn't mind. I got reclining seats in the car so what the hell, and it was dark–'

'The lights at the gate were out, then?'

Glanville nodded. 'I suppose so, 'cos it was dark in that lane.'

'What time was it then?'

'Can't be sure. After ten, certainly. But I didn't check. I just switched off the lights, turned on the radio for some sweet, soft music – and it gives a nice glow as well, kind of romantic, you know – and got stuck in. Great, I thought, because she was ... well, enthusiastic, you know?' He shook his head uncertainly. 'And then she just cooled, just like that.' He snapped his fingers disgustedly.

'She told us she had a bit of a tussle with you,' Crow said quietly.

'Now she can't come that one. All right, maybe her blouse got wrenched a bit, but I was ... niggled, you know? But I've never had to fight for it before, and I wasn't going to start then.' He glanced at the two detectives and his face became heavier, duller. 'So

179

I just let her out, had a fag and sat there for a while, then pushed off.'

'Did you see anyone in the lane while you were parked there?'

Glanville shook his head slowly. 'No... But there was someone coming out of the site when I left. I remember, I'd wound down the window, flicked my fag out, reached to turn on the radio and I heard someone running into the lane. I started the car and drove off – I just had the vague feeling maybe someone was after *me*, you know?'

Crow looked at Stafford. He raised his eyebrows. 'Why should you think that, Mr Glanville?'

Glanville was quiet for a moment. His eyebrows drew together in a protective ridge and he breathed heavily like a bull con-sidering a charge. 'Now look,' he said, with a defensive tone in his voice. 'I'm not ad-mitting I roughed up that woman. She led me on, I thought I was away, maybe I got insistent, but I didn't rough her up. Other fellers might have done so in the same circumstances, I tell you. But I didn't. Even so, when I heard someone running I thought it was time to leave. So I left.'

'I don't understand,' Crow said flatly.

Glanville expelled his breath gustily. 'I'll put it plain. She as good as told me, without words, that I could lay her. I was headed for it. Then she changed her mind. Okay, but I was burning! So I pushed her a bit, gave her a few choice words and off she went. Then I thought maybe her man was coming after me.'

'Why should you think that? Didn't she say she lived alone?' Stafford asked.

'Well, yes,' Glanville said, turning to look at Stafford. 'But she started to change her mind just after that guy passed us in the lane–'

'Someone *passed* you?'

Glanville was taken aback by the sharpness in Crow's tone. 'Didn't I say someone passed us? Someone did, but I didn't see who it was, I mean I was head down burrowing away and I wasn't worrying about other people outside the car. I'd locked the door, we had a fug going–'

'But Ruby cooled?'

'She *did*. She didn't say it was because she'd heard someone in the lane, but believe me, she was no longer interested in what I had to offer. We sat and argued maybe five minutes but she wanted out. I called her a few nasty names but I let her go, and I had a fag to get rid of my frustration. Then there was the running … and off I went.'

'What time would that be?' Crow asked.

'Eleven … maybe a few minutes earlier. I switched on the radio when I hit the main road and I got the time then. It was eleven o'clock.'

Crow grunted. He picked up his coffee and sipped at it. 'I thought you already had the radio on.'

For a moment Glanville looked puzzled, then the doubt faded from his eyes. 'That's right, I did ... the soft music, to get Ruby in the mood. Ah, yeah, I did put it on but that was for just a couple of minutes. You see, some joker broke across the music with nonsense about a battle in Stowford so I switched off. Besides, it wasn't really necessary, you know? Ruby didn't need the sweet music. She was hot for me, I could tell.'

'Until someone passed you in the lane.'

'That's it.'

'You didn't see the person who passed you, or which way he was going?' Stafford asked.

'Aw, come on, I was otherwise occupied! Me and Ruby was snuggled down, going great guns, or about to! But whoever it was, he was going away from the site.'

'*He?*' Crow asked.

'Or she. I just wouldn't know.'

Crow hesitated. 'You say that after that Ruby *cooled*. Did she look up when this person passed?'

Glanville licked his lips and made a doubtful gesture with his hand. 'Well, I can't rightly be certain – I was kind of ... *burrowing,* you know? But her face was above me, and I guess she could have seen, though with the fug we had going … but one thing was clear, it scared her right off.'

Crow looked at him sharply '*Scared* her?'

Glanville was startled. He glanced quickly at George Stafford and then back to Crow, as though he felt it was he who was about to be charged with the murder of Chuck Lindop. He fluttered his hands.

'Well, yes, didn't I make myself clear before? I tell you, we was going great, and it takes a lot to cool a woman off in that state. But one thing does it. I've had it happen before. There was a piece down in Broadstairs that I was with once when I really had to do the French farce bit, you know, hopping out of a window, and it was just like that. They freeze, man, their mouths go sort of open and loose and their eyes go wild. She was like that.'

'You didn't tell us.'

'No, well, in a way it was an impression I got at the time that sort of got … lost. I mean, there was this chap passing us, she started shaking, and I looked around, saw nothing for her to get worked up about and I suppose my own urgency got the better of my common sense. I wanted us to settle again, but she wanted out. And that made me mad. I mean I couldn't *see* anything to worry about.'

'But she *was* worried?'

'I reckon she was,' Glanville said. 'She'd

have been out of that car fast if I hadn't been grabbing her. I tell you, she really wanted *out...*'

After Glanville had gone, in rather subdued fashion, Crow and Stafford sat silently in their room. Stafford pointed out at last that Hartley had been waiting for well over an hour but Crow said the waiting would do him good. Stafford read over Glanville's statement as Crow checked it with Ruby's: they tallied. The couple had left Stowford just after ten, arrived at the site just after ten-fifteen, Ruby had left the car about ten-forty and Glanville had left just before eleven. But Ruby had made no mention of the man in the lane. Glanville said he remembered the time because Ruby had asked him to check it when they arrived at the site, but Ruby made no mention of that. More importantly, she made no mention of her sudden, and, if Glanville's impressions were to be given credence, frightened cooling. Crow stared at the statement, then took Glanville's statement and read through that.

There was something there that bothered him. Something at the back of his mind. The man in the lane? Someone walking away from the site at ten thirty-five? Or something else, something irrelevant at first sight but *important,* nevertheless.

He sighed. It was gone. Best to leave it.

2

There were some people the gods never favoured. They were small when all around them were tall. They lacked confidence when others brimmed over with it; they were followers when others were leaders; they had mean, lined faces when others had open countenances that could be a positive asset in life. The man who sat looking at the floor in front of John Crow was such a man. He was just five feet four inches tall, fifty years old and no matter how much he paid for his clothes he always looked ill-dressed. His skin was grey and patchy, what little hair he had was thin, and drawn forward in a vain attempt to hide the extending bald patch in the front. The only remarkable thing about him was his eyes. They hardly seemed to fit in his mean, wizened face. They were brown and soft, intelligence gleamed out of them, but an intelligence stained with cunning. They were not nice eyes, but they were not *bad* eyes; they darted glances that were like the flash of a pike after a stickleback, acquisitive and hungry, but they had a hurt in them too, a deep dissatisfaction with life and the way it had treated their owner. Fifty years of age, and here again, in front of the police. It was neverending, it would never end. His lean fingers picked at the button of his jacket, never still; he did not look up when Crow spoke at last.

'Inspector Stafford, I'll have to tell you about Mr *Hartley*.'

Crow leaned back in his chair and smiled. He shook his head, ran one hand over its baldness, and clucked his tongue.

'We'll settle for Mr Hartley, since he seems to want to be known by that name, but I've known him for years as Frederick Hartley Semmings. Isn't that right, Fred?'

The little man flicked a quick, plaintive glance in Stafford's direction but said nothing. Crow smiled again.

'Don't be misled by his meekness, Inspector Stafford – not until you've heard about Fred. I met him first – when was it, Fred? Twenty years ago? When you were first put inside? The thing is, Fred's got a record, almost as long as the rope he used to use as a cat. A man of parts, our Fred. He started life as a locksmith's apprentice, fell in with the wrong crowd, started opening doors, getting in through windows and then graduated to roofs. One of the most successful cat burglars in London at one time. There was a five-year spell when he almost made the top flight, so to speak. Isn't that so, Fred?'

'That's all in the past, Mr Crow,' the little man pleaded.

'Maybe so,' Crow said. The smile faded

from his lips, and he stared at Hartley dispassionately. 'The trouble was you were always a bad picker, weren't you? You used to pick the wrong roof, the wrong house, the wrong companions. There was always something to go *wrong*.'

The narrow shoulders lifted despondently. 'I never had the luck, Mr Crow.'

'A good cat needs the luck,' Crow said in a soft voice. 'How many years in the last thirty have been spent inside, Fred?'

Hartley didn't want to say the word but it struggled out as though it were determined to emerge in spite of him. 'Twelve,' he said.

Stafford grunted. 'Unlucky is the word!'

'You'll appreciate my surprise,' Crow remarked, 'when I came face to face with my old friend Fred Hartley Semmings at Lovesome Hill.' He waited for a moment, then added, 'Have you thought over what I said yesterday, Fred?'

Hartley shook his narrow head unhappily. His fingers picked an anxious pattern over his jacket as he said, 'I don't think you got what I was trying to say to you, Mr Crow. I'm *retired*.'

'Villains don't retire,' Crow said, 'except into the nick.'

'Really,' Hartley protested. 'I mean it, Mr Crow. You got to understand the way it's been with me. Thirty years I been doin' jobs, I freely admit it–'

'You've got no choice. Your form is well known.'

'All right, but things is different now. I changed. I retired. I … well, to give it to you straight, Mr Crow, I pulled a job about three years ago that gave me a bigger haul than anything I ever did before. I'm not going to tell you what it is, naturally, but for a while I thought it was going to be the one that would put me in the big time. Give me … *recognition*.'

Stafford's mouth was open. Crow smiled at him as Hartley paused, then went on, seemingly oblivious.

'There wasn't a copper in London got the knot on me; the lift was one where the sufferer couldn't squeal; I tell you, Mr Crow, it was a good job, and I was about to get respect. Then–'

'As usual,' Crow said drily.

'Like you said, as usual, things went wrong. There was this bird–'

'There's always a bird.'

'She took me, fleeced me, everything except a couple of thousand I'd stashed away for a rainy day. So I decided I'd retire, get out while the going's good. I looked around, found the bungalow up at Lovesome Hill, it was in a rough state, I been two years putting it to rights, and here I am.'

'Retired,' Crow said.

'That's it.'

'I don't believe you,' Crow said coldly.

Hartley spread his hands and looked despondent but not surprised; with his luck would anyone ever believe him? He glanced towards Stafford to make his point but Stafford just grinned at him.

'We're investigating a murder case, Mr Hartley.'

'Now wait a minute.' Life was injected into Hartley's cold veins. He sat up, looked around him as though he could already see the walls of a prison cell closing in on him. 'Let's get this straight. I never got involved with any heavy stuff in my life.'

'There's always a first time.'

'Not for me. Not with murder!'

'So it's just coincidence you happened to be up at Lovesome Hill, a man with a record as long as my arm, not fifty yards from the spot where a man got murdered the other night?'

'I swear!' Hartley was agitated, almost bouncing in his chair. 'Coincidence, believe me. Unlucky I've been, but never so unlucky as to get tied up with *murder!*'

'So let's talk about burglary, then,' Crow said affably.

Fred Hartley Semmings opened his mouth and shut it again slowly. A vein beat steadily in his narrow temple and his eyes flickered away from Crow's to study the floor intently. He had the feeling he had suddenly been trapped into an admission even though he had made none; it was as though he had been built up, scared into the thought of having to face an unwarranted murder charge, and now the other, lesser thing, seemed almost welcome. It was old, familiar ground and he felt safer on it.

'I told you, Mr Crow. I retired.'

'And I told you I didn't believe you,' Crow said cheerfully. 'Tell me about Cobham Park, Fred.'

'Cobham Park? You *must* be joking! I had nothing to do with that mess!'

'How did you know it was a mess?' Crow asked quietly.

Hartley's glance came up this time, and he stared at Crow unwinkingly. He seemed to be calculating chances, weighing the odds. He pursed his lips. 'You know how we pros look at things. Anything I'm not involved in is bound to be a mess.'

'Won't do, Fred. I want real answers. I told you last night. You've been sitting too close to a field where a murder took place. I don't like coincidences and I don't believe in them. I gave you last night to sweat it out of your own system; if it isn't coming out, then I'll sweat it out of you.' Crow frowned suddenly. 'You know me, Fred. You know I mean what I say. You know I can make life bloody difficult for you, I can tag every step you make, I can harass you from breakfast-time till supper-time and drag you out of bed in the middle of the night. I can send you back to the Smoke, and I can put you inside. I could make sure we find something on you today and put you before the beaks; with your record you wouldn't stand a chance.'

'You wouldn't do that, Mr Crow.' Hartley's eyes were glittering now. 'You wouldn't plant stuff on me.'

'Not if you started answering me honestly. But play silly buggers with me, and I'll do likewise with you.'

Hartley licked his lips. He seemed almost to have forgotten Stafford's presence. He pondered on Crow's words, chewed them over, and his eyes were fixed on Crow's cold face.

'Cobham Park,' he said at last.

'Tell me,' Crow said.

'I was offered… The place had been cased, there was jewellery in there, I was told. I went out one night on my own, took a look, saw it was an easy enough pull … but I didn't like it. So I backed out. I swear, Mr Crow, I had nothing to do with that lift. It was a messy, bungled job – they didn't get nothing out of it, and they *carved* their way in. Any alarm system would have cooked for them, but they were lucky and got out – even if they didn't get much loot.'

'So who was it?'

'Aw, come on, Mr Crow, you don't expect me to shop them!'

Crow rose slowly and walked across to the window. The pavements were dry now, the sun bright on the rooftops. The Broadway was quietly busy, people shopping, women gossiping, as though the fair had never been, as though a man hadn't been killed out at Lovesome Hill. Without turning, he said quietly, 'There was an occasion once, over the Fulford Hill robbery, when you came to see me, Fred.'

There was a short silence.

'That was different, Mr Crow.'

'You wanted a favour.'

'And I paid for it–'

'By shopping Macmillan. Oh, I know you could square that with your conscience, but that's not my problem. What I do know is this: once a man turns snout, he can do it again. And will. You know what I thought when I saw you yesterday, Fred? First thing that flashed through my mind? Call it intuition, but it snapped right at me. Fred Hartley Semmings, I thought – and *Northleach Hall*. It would be a big job, a job for Fred. And that's why you're here now, one of the reasons, anyway. Northleach would be your style, and the London mob's not prowling this area. There's no experienced cats around here, not like you; even if you are over fifty you can still show them a thing or two.'

'No, Mr Crow. I told you, I'm retired.'

'The hell you are!'

'Truth, Mr Crow.' Hartley looked up at Crow as he turned from the window. 'I swear. I *couldn't* do Northleach any more than I could do Cobham Park. *I got a dicky heart.*'

He'd always been unlucky, Fred Hartley Semmings. And this had been the last of the blows Fate was dealing him. A successful burglar needed nerve, and he needed a pulse that ran steady and true. A good lifter needed to be calm and easy – and light on his feet if trouble came his way. But the life must have been over for Fred the day he was told.

'Tell me, Fred,' Crow said, and sat down with his elbows on his knees.

'Not much to tell,' Hartley said despondently. The resistance seemed to have drained out of him now. 'Five years ago I did a job – the one I told you about, only it wasn't so big. On the way back I had to scarper a bit, and I ended up pretty breathless. First time I noticed. Six months later I sat down in the street. Just sat down. Like someone hit me in the chest. Could hardly breathe for the pain. And I couldn't speak. That scared me, not being able to speak. So I saw the doc.'

'What was the verdict?'

'He said I'd been *lucky!* I mean to say, lucky! Asked me what job I did, told him I was a clerk, he said fine, you'll live to a ripe old age, if you take it easy. I almost laughed in his face. Until the next time, when I slid through a window and almost never got out again. That was it, Mr Crow, believe me. I took what I had, fenced it, and got out of the Smoke. I needed a quiet life – it had to be a quiet life. It was that, or the long sleep!'

'That's why you turned down Cobham Park?' Crow asked.

Hartley nodded. 'Oh, I was tempted, you got to understand that. When I got the tickle I agreed to look the place over, and I did. It was easy. I could have done it – but I didn't dare. So help me, Mr Crow, I *wanted* to but I couldn't. I'm ready to admit the wanting, but you must understand, it could have put me in the cemetery. So I refused, I backed out, they did it, and they made a mess of it.'

'All right, Fred, let's get on with the rest of it. Northleach Hall.'

Hartley licked his lips. He raised his left hand and began to massage his chest with a light pressure, as though reminding himself of reasons and excuses.

'I got approached again.'

'And said no, for the same reasons?'

'For the same reasons. But they kept on … and then, well, I guessed how I could take the heat off myself.'

Crow nodded. 'You rang the police.'

'You got to understand, Mr Crow,' Hartley insisted with a hint of torn pride. 'I'm no snout. That Macmillan thing, that was different, I needed a favour and you got to buy favours from coppers, even coppers like you. And this was different too. I was under pressure, you understand. He said he *wanted* me; said the first job got screwed up because I wasn't there to help out. This time I *had* to go. So I agreed; I played for time; and then I made that call. It was a way of stopping it before it ever got started. And there'd be no way of knowing I'd grassed. It would just be that the job wasn't on any more because the police were nosing around. It was safe, and it was foolproof.'

'Who was it, Fred? Who was it pressured you over Cobham Park and Northleach?'

The words came out unwillingly, like a spoon from thick treacle. It almost hurt Hartley physically to speak.

'Chuck Lindop. It was that bastard Lindop.'

3

In the late afternoon John Crow went back to his room at the hotel and took a bath. He had left Fred Hartley Semmings with Stafford, making his statement, checking it, signing it. Fred was not averse to staying at the station overnight; in fact, he almost seemed to want it. He was nervous, and he was scared – and he had reason to be. While he dressed, Crow thought back over what Fred had said.

'Lindop was a real bastard. He knew how to put the screws on a man. I met him first in a pub at Stowford – he came up to me, said he knew me, and he did too, God knows how, though he said he had contacts in the Smoke and I'd been pointed out to him once when he was a kid, and what a coincidence we should meet like that in Stowford. I let him rattle on, didn't mind 'cos he was buying, you know, and then suddenly I began to get his drift. He was sounding me out about a job.'

The mere thought of the conversation with Lindop had twisted Fred's mouth as he recounted it to Crow.

'He tried to tell me he was big time, experienced, said he'd done more than a few heists in his time, but believe me, Mr Crow, I *knew* he was an amateur. The pros, the real pros, they don't need to talk like that, and they don't need to winkle out old deadbeats like me. No, the fact was Lindop wanted to do a lift but he wanted me to be there – and I told him flat. He could go to hell.' Fred's eyes narrowed thoughtfully. 'You know, he just laughed? Laughed, went away, didn't see him for a couple of weeks and then he called at the bungalow. He told me this was my last chance, he had a job fixed, Cobham Park, and he wanted me in. I refused. So off he went. I took a look at the place out of interest like I told you, but I wasn't involved. Next thing I heard, it had been done, rough job, and no real gravy at the end of it. That'll teach him, I thought.'

He shook his head slowly from side to side, as though regretting his own foolishness.

'Maybe I should have up and left then, instead of staying around, but I told him, I was *retired*. So why couldn't he leave me alone? But he didn't. He called around again, very cool, but nasty. He gave it to me straight. *He* had no record, he said. No one would ever put Cobham Park on his back. But I was different. One word to the local coppers and they'd be down on my neck like a pack of hounds. They'll never give you a moment's peace again, he told me. They'll be harrying you, dragging you in for questioning every time anything happens in the neighbourhood. They'll make your life a misery, he said. But I still said I could face that. It was then that Chuck Lindop turned real ugly. He put it to me straight. He said he'd got another place cased and it was going to be a dawdle – to a man of my experience. It was Northleach Hall, and the end of the rainbow would be golden. I just laughed at him, you know, Mr Crow? Then he stood up and he grabbed me, lifted me off my feet.'

There was a hint of panic in Fred's eyes even then as he told Crow about the incident.

'He shoved his face into mine, Mr Crow, and his eyes was sort of glintin' as red as that bloody hair of his. He looked kind of mad, you know what I mean? He said there wouldn't be just the coppers to contend with, if I didn't come in with him. He had oppoes in the village, and nights got dark, and a man with a dicky heart could easily get scared to *death* and find himself in a ditch one lonely night and no one the wiser. It was a promise, he said; if I didn't tie in over Northleach Hall he'd shove me into hell and there wouldn't be a mark on me. He scared me, Mr Crow, I don't mind admitting it. He scared me stiff.'

'So you agreed to go in with him?'

Fred Hartley Semmings nodded jerkily. 'That's right. I cased the place with him, agreed on the lift, but all the time I was scared. I was mad too, because he was *forcing* me to do something I knew I couldn't – or at least shouldn't – do with my ticker. But you see how it was? Either way, I could be for the high jump!'

'You could have gone to the police.'

'Aw, come on, Mr Crow! All right, I did for Macmillan but that was different, and that was with *you*. And you wasn't around here just then, and besides, if I'd gone to the inspector here, what would have happened? I had no *proof* Lindop did Cobham Park; it was my word against his about Northleach Hall; he had no record like me; I'd have to let on who I was and you both know what that would have meant; there would have been the chance I wouldn't have been believed – and after all that, what would have happened? If Lindop stood up under questioning you'd have had to release him, and then one night I'd have been found under a hedge with a bloody terrified look on my face, cold as mutton on a Monday morning. It just wasn't on, Mr Crow, it just wasn't *on*.'

'So you managed a compromise?'

'That was it exactly! If I couldn't go straight to the coppers there was one other way around it. If I did a bit of snouting, rang Stowford and told them that Northleach had been cased, there was the chance the heat would make Lindop have second thoughts about the job, maybe even drop the whole idea. All right, it was snouting, but what the hell? I was trying to save my *skin*, Mr Crow.'

'Did it work?'

Fred's mouth drooped. 'Maybe. I'm not sure. I mean, it was pretty obvious he knew the police were on to something but he never let on he suspected I'd grassed. I'm pretty sure he hadn't called it off, but he was getting edgy about it. So I made a second call, just to hurry things along, convince him it was a no go. That way maybe I'd get off the hook, if only for a while.'

'And did that work? Did Lindop call it off?'

Fred's face tightened and the panic came back into his eyes. 'No, he didn't call it off. It no longer became possible for him. He got topped… And maybe I'd have been glad about it, because it meant I would have been let off that bloody Northleach hook. But in fact, the way it worked out was worse… Mr Crow, you got to give me some assurances, right now. What I got to say, it's got to give me the right to some protection. The fact is if I was scared by Chuck Lindop I've been more bloody scared since.'

'Tell us, Fred,' Crow had said softly.

'Lindop could be rough; I could see that in his eyes, in the way that red hair flared when he got stroppy. But he always had a bit of calculation in him, you know? He was always weighing chances, and if the trouble wasn't worth it he'd back off. But this other man – he's different. He's thicker than Lindop ever was, but he's meaner too. And he scares me. Crazy men, they *always* scare me.'

'You've been threatened again?'

'I was threatened the night Chuck Lindop got killed. It was the same old story –

200

Northleach Hall was still on, and to hell with the risks. But that's what I mean, you see – I was worse off. Now I had to contend with *this* crazy bastard!'

It was five-thirty by the time Crow was ready to leave his hotel. He had dismissed the driver, and took the squad car alone once more. There had been a great deal of sense in what Fred Hartley Semmings had stated: the word of an acknowledged burglar didn't carry much weight. But John Crow had a good idea where he might be able to obtain some necessary corroboration.

He drove slowly to Lovesome Hill Caravan Park. A much clearer picture of the night's events was now emerging. The statements of Andrew Keene, Sara Keene, Ruby Sanders, Forsyth and the others were now on file and the salient facts from each were locked away in his brain. As he drove he was able to sift through them again, going over facts, checking movements and times. It was all beginning to fit; he needed just a few more facts, and then the job would be done.

Yet there was still something fluttering away at the back of his mind, like a piece of paper caught on a bush on a windy day; he could see it, but he could not read it, and it bothered him. But it would become clearer – if he waited, didn't agonize about it, it would come clearer. Woods and trees, as Martha said on such occasions, woods and trees, and matches. He didn't know what she meant, but she said it with such a satisfied air that he never liked to ask her.

Crow reached the caravan park at five forty-five. He parked inside the gateway, and glanced briefly at the generator: they had wondered about that man Dixon, but the ways things were going now he doubted Dixon would be charged with much apart from malicious damage. He turned and walked down the site towards the trees. Out of the corner of his eye he saw movement in one van down the site as he bore left towards the clump of trees.

He made his way into the wood. The undergrowth dragged at his legs, brambles and blackberry thickets pulled at him. He searched for a few minutes as the sunlight filtering through the branches above his head dappled the ground, and at last he found the area with the sadly small patch of freshly turned earth. He stood there, staring at it, waiting.

Within a few minutes he heard what he expected – someone walking into the wood behind him. He did not turn around, for he knew who it would be. The footsteps stopped behind him, some ten feet or more. Silence came back under the trees, except for an occasional scurrying sound as a blackbird threshed its way among low-lying branches and leaves.

'What are you looking for?' Ruby Sanders asked in a nervous voice.

John Crow turned his head slowly and looked at her. She was dressed soberly, for her: a plain white blouse with no frills, dark blue, tight trousers flared at the ankles. She wore no make-up and curiously enough it made her seem younger even though there were lines to be observed around her eyes. Perhaps it was not youth but an essential innocence that the make-up normally obscured; Crow could not be sure. But there was no mistaking the anxiety that shadowed her eyes and the nervousness that had brought her into the woods.

'This is where you buried your dog, isn't it?' Crow asked.

'Andrew … Andrew did it for me,' she said nodding, her eyes bright with sudden tears.

'You said Patch was knocked down by a car.'

Again she nodded. Crow watched her carefully. 'Andrew didn't see the dog. You had it in a box. He just buried the box.'

She made no reply, but the brightness of her eyes had gone again to be replaced by the anxiety. She ran a pink tongue over dry lips. 'I'm just beginning to wonder whether there really is a dog in that box,' Crow said.

Ruby Sanders was taken aback. She looked

around her, her mouth opening and shutting in surprise. 'What on earth do you mean?'

Crow turned away and looked at the patch of earth. 'It's just a supposition on my part. You see, I've spoken to Mrs Lindop, and I understand that Chuck Lindop had something deposited at a hotel not too far from here. Now *someone* emptied the deposit box immediately after Lindop's death. It just occurred to me that with this box being buried–'

'You must be mad!'

Crow looked at her dispassionately. 'It's just a hunch I had. You wouldn't object to my getting some officers down to turn up the box, have a look inside it?'

Ruby's face stiffened. The anxiety turned to panic and she looked down at the patch of earth as though it held unnamed terrors. 'I ... I don't see why you want to ... you can't go turning...'

'Why not?' Crow asked quietly. 'What objection could you possibly have? If there's just the body of a dog in there, killed by a car, it's a gruesome task for my men, but that shouldn't worry you. Why do you object?'

Ruby began to shake. It was a combination of fear and distress. 'I just don't want you to ... to open Patch's grave. I swear to you that's all there is in there – Patch. Nothing else.'

'We'll be careful,' Crow said. 'But we need to check.'

Ruby clenched her fist, looked over her shoulder back towards the site. Please, don't go digging him up. Leave him alone now, leave him alone. I promise you, it's only Patch in there.'

'I know it,' Crow said soberly.

For a moment she hardly seemed to hear him, or if she did, was unable to comprehend his meaning. Then suddenly her head shot around and she glared at him. 'You *know* it?'

Crow nodded. 'I don't really think there's anything buried in there apart from the dog. But I wanted to see what your reaction would be if I suggested exhumation.'

'I ... I don't understand.'

'I think you do.' Crow hesitated. 'I wondered if you'd react violently to my suggestion. You did. It confirms in my mind a suspicion I've had. Tell me, Ruby, if my men dig in that grave and find Patch, will they find blood? Will they find a dog's body squashed by the wheels of a car? Or will they find something else? Patch, unmarked perhaps, but with poison in his stomach? Or maybe not even that. More likely, perhaps, his head twisted at an odd angle. Is that what they'd find, Ruby?'

Ruby's face was white. She rocked on her heels, staggered slightly, then turned and set

205

off at a blind, desperate run back through the wood as though seeking escape from truths that faced her. Crow watched her go, a stumbling, frightened woman, suddenly very small and vulnerable, and very scared. She fought her way past the trees as though she expected them to grab at her, hold her back, and when she lurched into the camp site itself she almost fell. Then she was running back down towards her van, heedlessly, with her hands on her mouth. Unbalanced, she seemed to be waddling down across the turf, ungainly, her short legs splayed as she ran, her tight trousered bottom absurd in its jouncing. She had lost all her sexuality, the picture she presented was a pathetic one. Crow felt sorry for her, and the knowledge that he was partly responsible for her distress and was now about to take advantage of it brought an ache that was almost physical inside him. It was a familiar enough feeling and one he should have got over years ago, but he knew he never would. And in his quieter moments he admitted to himself that if he ever did lose that feeling – compassion – he would want to be dead. More slowly than Ruby, he made his way out of the wood and walked down towards her caravan.

He tapped lightly on the door and entered even though she had not invited him in. She had been crying, but the tears had stopped.

From time to time she gave a shudder, as though sobs came up from her chest, uncontrollable, but her features were a mask of indifference – the anxiety, the fear, the distress seemed to have gone. Crow knew it was only a mask. Underneath, Ruby Sanders would be feeling raw and exposed and scared. But also, perhaps, aware she was cornered.

'Are you all right?' Crow asked. 'Well enough to talk to me, I mean?'

She did not look at him. Her eyes were fixed on the window, but she was seeing nothing external to herself. The images on her retinas were old images, dredged up from inside herself, and he suspected they would be older than her involvement with Chuck Lindop. But it was that which he wished to bring forward to her consciousness.

'I'd better tell you what I know,' he said regretfully, 'so you can understand where we are. I already know a great deal about the last few months, and all I want from you is corroboration. I think I can find some up there in the woods but it wouldn't be conclusive. But *you* can fix things for me, Ruby.'

He paused, but Ruby Sanders made no sign that she had ever heard him. After a moment John Crow went on, staring at his linked bony fingers. 'We now have a statement from Fred Hartley, who's been living up at the bungalow above the site. And it helps fill in the picture of Chuck Lindop, and a little more. What it amounts to is this. Lindop was a small-time, vicious womanizer who had ideas that he could haul himself up the criminal ladder by using information he had acquired about people. He could never see that he was a small man essentially; his ideas were grand. He was indulging in petty theft, working small fraudulent schemes to make a little money on the side, but he saw himself as having the ability to make a big pull – at Cobham Park.'

The images Ruby was seeing had begun to change. At his words, she was beginning to come alive again.

'Lindop was pressing Fred Hartley to join him in the Cobham Park burglary. But he also told Hartley he had two other accomplices. One of these was not unlike Lindop himself. The other Hartley did not know. Fred Hartley took no part in Cobham Park and it was a fiasco. Lindop was angry so really put pressure on him. It ended – or *should* have ended – when Chuck Lindop died. But it didn't. Instead, Hartley found himself still under pressure, and worse than before. Because Lindop's accomplice came to him and said it was still on: he'd use the same lever on Hartley, and if he didn't come in there'd be trouble. Not just exposure to the police, but real trouble. Physical trouble. For while Lindop may have been content with just threats, this man was different. He was violent by nature, stupid, unthinking, dangerous and violent. He scared Hartley to hell, and Hartley agreed to do it.'

Ruby was listening now. Her glance had moved away from the window and she was looking at Crow. The colour had begun to come back to her cheeks.

'I've talked to your salesman, Glanville,' Crow said. 'Hartley tells me that he was pressured into agreeing to continue with Northleach Hall on the very night that Lindop died. And the man putting the pressure on *knew* Lindop was dead. Yet the time was still only about ten forty-five. Glanville tells me that you and he were snuggling down quite nicely until you suddenly cooled – *when someone passed you in the lane.* Now then, Ruby, I think you saw the man in the lane, recognized him, got scared because you were in the car with Glanville and got the hell out of there as quickly as you could. I think you hurried back on to the site and joined the Keenes in their van. But later, when the questions arose in your mind, you were foolish, and you put them. The result was Patch died...'

She moved her lips, staring at Crow.

'I want to know who that man in the lane was,' Crow said fiercely. 'I am pretty sure I know his name already, but I want to know. Who was he, and in which direction was he walking?'

She seemed almost relieved to whisper the name.

'It was Hoagy. He was walking up the lane – away from the site.'

CHAPTER VI

1

She leaned her head back against the window. Her face was tired and resigned. She lifted a hand to her hair, touching it as though it were the one stable thing in her existence, and in a way it was, still stiff, unmoving, undisturbed by the running away and the terror and the death that swirled around her. Emotional stress, the death of her dog Patch, the murder of Chuck Lindop, it had all touched her, shaken her. But now it was over, Crow could see it in her resignation. She knew that Crow was reaching out to the truth – and she had less need to fear Hogarth Samson.

'I never really liked him,' she said. 'Not even at the beginning. But it was a ... delicate time for me, you know what I mean? I was feeling a bit raw, the way Chuck had thrown me over, and Hoagy was around. I mean, he was a big man, and he was *interested* in me at a time I was feeling low, and he was good in bed... So he moved in and took up where Chuck left off and that was okay for a while.'

She shook her head, staring out of the window fixedly as though looking for the reasons and the motivations out there in the trees where Patch lay buried. 'But I never liked him. Chuck Lindop, now, he was rough, he could frighten you because he was hard and he was a bastard but there was a difference between him and Hoagy. There'd come a point when Chuck would weigh up the chances and say to hell with it, it's not worth going on for the trouble it would cause. But Hoagy was never like that. He's rough and he's a bastard like Chuck but he never gives up. He ploughs on, unminding. Like you said, stupid, and dangerous.'

'Why didn't you get rid of him?' Crow asked quietly.

Ruby lifted her shoulders in a deprecating gesture. 'You just don't know what it's like. In this world, if you live alone with no one around, what choice do you have? I did try to break away from him, not long after we got started. I'd healed over Chuck, I'd had enough of Hoagy, and I picked up a barman in Stowford. Not because I was struck on him, just a way of getting adrift of Hoagy. I stayed the night with the feller – next evening, after stop tap, he was putting some crates out behind the pub and he got clobbered. Just a couple of blows, but it broke two ribs for him, and smashed in his nose, so he took the hint. So did I, at two o'clock the same morning.'

She hesitated, then reached for the top button of her blouse. She undid it, moved on to the other buttons. Crow watched her. It was a curious performance, devoid of sexuality; he could have been a doctor, her movements were meaningless. She pulled the blouse off her shoulders, unhooked her brassiere to partly expose her left breast. 'Look,' she said flatly.

The bruises were perhaps a week old, yellowing and fading, but clearly imprinted by the fingertips that had caused them. The marks on her upper arm were bad enough but there was a long bruise running down to the side of the breast that showed the deliberateness of Samson's viciousness.

'Never my face,' she said. 'But my body...' She dressed again quickly, as though she were suddenly aware that Crow was a man and she had regained some of her lost innocence. 'Oh, he didn't love me or anything mushy like that but I was here, easy, convenient, regular. I was his woman, he owned me and *he'd* call it a day, not me. But there was another side to it as well: the funny thing is, Hoagy knew he was different from Chuck, and knew Chuck was ... well, superior. Hoagy wanted to be like Chuck. You said Lindop was small – well, maybe he was. But he was bigger than Hoagy and Hoagy wanted to grow. That's one of the reasons why he picked me up when Chuck dropped me. Call it stupid, but you've said he is – the fact of the matter is that he scared the hell out of me, I did what he wanted, *when* he wanted, and there was no more running off – while he seemed to think that by having me he was following Chuck and some of Chuck would rub off on him. At the same time, he seemed to feel he was getting one up on Chuck too, having the woman Chuck had thrown aside, though Chuck didn't see it like that – and Chuck didn't touch me after Hoagy came around. Like I was tainted or something.'

There was no bitterness in her tone. She was being factual, and honest.

'Anyway, to cut a long story short there I was with Hoagy coming down like a randy bull whenever he felt like it… One thing he did have in common with Chuck was he'd talk in bed. Boast, is a better word. I knew about Cobham Park soon enough and I heard about Northleach too. Chuck and Hoagy, they were going to strong-arm their way into the money by breaking in at Cobham and they were going to get Fred Hartley to help them. There was someone else involved too, but I never quite got to know about that. Anyway, Hoagy told me Chuck and he had it all worked out–'

'Did he ever talk about money that Chuck Lindop had hidden away?'

Ruby nodded. 'From time to time, when

he was drunk, he'd moan about the fact he reckoned Chuck had a mint stashed away and he'd like to get his hands on it. I thought it was just talk. I couldn't see Chuck ever building up a real pile.'

'All right, now tell me about the night Lindop died.'

Ruby shook her head as though she had some difficulty in clearing it. 'You know, there's not a lot I can tell you about it. I still don't understand what got into me – any more than I can understand this last day or so. That night, Hoagy had pushed off into town to meet some of his gipsy friends – he has a streak of Romany himself, you know? I sat back here, and I had a few drinks, and there was hardly anyone on the site and I got bloody resentful. Was I supposed to sit there while everyone was off having a good time? Anyway, fortified by some Dutch courage I took the bus into Stowford. It was there I picked up this Jimmie guy – Glanville you called him? He was all right. He brought me back. I wasn't fussy – I'd had a few drinks and he seemed harmless enough and I guessed Hoagy would be in town till the early hours. He usually was. Anyway, there we was for a while and he was just getting down to business when I heard someone in the lane. I looked out – couldn't see too well because of the fug on the windows, but I got to thinking it could be

Hoagy. And that *scared* me. I'd asked Jimmie about the time earlier and he'd seemed a bit vague, said his watch was playing up; so right now I began to get worried. The thing was, I could have been wrong, Hoagy could have come back earlier and found my van empty. That scared me. I had visions of that barman and I could see Hoagy spreading this chap Jimmie all over the lane. And worse – he'd lay into me too, good and proper. That sobered me up rapidly, I can tell you. So as Glanville fumbled away I took a good look out and saw this man – and it looked like Hoagy – entering Hartley's bungalow. The light shone from the doorway, I saw that much. And it was enough for me. I guessed I was best off back at the van. I felt I'd be safer there. So I hopped out after Jimmie had done a bit of swearing, torn my blouse and got clobbered with my shoe; I made my way back, heard Sara crying and sort of forgot my own problems then. Well, by going in to Sara I guess it also helped provide me with a sort of alibi too – if Hoagy had been looking for me at my van I could say I'd been with the Keenes.'

'Can you tell me what time it was when you saw Samson going to Hartley's bungalow?' Crow asked.

Ruby hesitated, biting her lip thoughtfully. 'Not really. It would be about ten thirty-five or ten-forty. I mean, I was anxious to get the hell out of there with that salesman trying still to crawl over me and time was the last thing I had on my mind. But I was with the Keenes for about ten minutes and then Andrew went up to the bungalow to make the phone call and he made it about eleven, wasn't that so?'

Crow nodded in agreement. 'Go on.'

'There's not a great deal more to tell. At first, I was sensible. Your people came around, and I didn't say anything, except the straightforward stuff. Hoagy didn't let on that he'd been at the site that evening and Hartley wasn't on the point of saying so either, so I shut up. I mean, in my position, what would you have done?'

'Maybe I would have done the same thing, Ruby,' Crow said quietly. The momentary defiance that had started to sparkle in her eyes faded and she shrugged.

'Fact is, I was scared. If I had said any-thing to you people the burglaries would come out, and then I didn't know what the hell Hoagy had been doing on the site that night, and there could be bad trouble in it all. So I kept quiet. But then … well, like I said, I still don't understand what got into me. I mean, charging off to Stowford that night was bad enough – *asking* for trouble. But then–'

Fear was staining her eyes again and she began to shake lightly, tremulously. After a moment Crow put out his hand, held hers tightly. There was a brief hesitation, then her fingers gripped his in return.

'I must have been crazy,' she said, in a voice dropping almost to a whisper. 'But there were so many things buzzing around in my head. Hoagy scared the pants off me, but I wanted to *know*. Was it him in the lane? What was he doing on the site? And maybe most of all I wanted to know if he had hammered Chuck. Funny thing, Mr Crow, I never had a down on Chuck, even after the way he treated me. He could make you feel...'

She released Crow's hand suddenly and turned away.

'The other night Hoagy came back slewed. He came to the van, tried to make it but he was too damned drunk. I sat there looking at him and I was so scared but so disgusted too. And suddenly I felt so bloody *clever*. I thought I could get it over the big oaf, maybe use it as a lever to get away from him. It was stupid and mixed up, but it seemed right at the time. He was half-asleep and very drunk and I asked him some stupid questions. He didn't really answer them, just mumbled, turned over and went to sleep. But next morning he was pretty quiet. I caught him looking at me oddly. And I felt as though my guts had been kicked in; I was shivering. But it was worse when he showed me ... showed me Patch.' Her face was stiff but her eyes were deep pools of horror. *He'd broken his neck.* Just like that. And he said he'd do the same to me if he ever had cause. And then he walked away.'

Stupid and dangerous, Crow thought as the horror in Ruby's eyes found a reflective movement in his stomach.

'You said you asked him some stupid questions. What were they?'

'The obvious ones. What time did he get back to the site the night Chuck was killed? Did he come on the bus? Did he and Chuck have a quarrel? Was the lift at Northleach Hall still on now that Chuck was dead? Like I said, he didn't answer them.'

Crow watched Ruby carefully. She did not seem to be disseminating, and shaken as she was it was likely she was now being candid, holding nothing back.

'What do *you* think happened that night, Ruby?' he asked quietly.

'I don't know, and I don't want to know. I've told you what I saw. It's your job to make something of it, not mine. All I want is for you to promise me you'll keep Hoagy away from me. If he ever found out that I'd talked to you—'

'He won't find out... Ruby, tell me this. Chuck Lindop dropped you months ago. There was nothing of the monk in his make-up. He found another woman?'

'He always found another woman,' she said, with a shrug. 'He needed women; when he dropped one there was always another being hunted. For a while, here on the site I wondered...' She frowned. 'Sometimes they lasted a week, sometimes months. Me, I lasted three months. But there was always someone.'

'One woman was called Dixon.'

Ruby stared at Crow woodenly. 'I live and let live.'

'Did you know about her?' Crow persisted.

She lifted a reluctant shoulder. 'I knew about her. Her old man kicked her out after he found out Chuck had been messing around with her.'

'How did Lindop come to meet Mrs Dixon?'

'Stowford. In a pub, with her old man, I think. Chuck and Sam Dixon were playing darts, he met her then.'

'Did Dixon and Lindop often play darts together?' Crow asked.

A slight frown creased Ruby's brow. She shook her head. 'No, of course not. Chuck wasn't a darts man. I think he had a game with Dixon just so's they could get talking, he could buy Mrs Dixon a drink, make her acquaintance. Why do you ask?'

'They didn't spend much time in each other's company – Sam Dixon and Lindop?'

'I don't *know*. He never came out here, that's for sure. But whether Sam Dixon was ever tied in much with Chuck, I wouldn't know. Is it important?'

Crow shrugged non-committally. It was not something he could really discuss with Ruby Sanders. But the fact was that it had probably been Sam Dixon who had blown the generator. It was likely to have been an act of revenge against Lindop for seducing his wife. But it *could* have been more: it could have been a way of getting darkness to the site, of luring Lindop up to the gate for an attack in the dark ... but then why was Lindop killed at his van? Apart from that, there was the other thought drifting around in his head. It was possible Sam Dixon had more than just one motive for getting at Chuck Lindop. Ruby and Hartley both said there had been another person involved with Samson and Lindop – Hartley to help with the break-in, and someone else. Could it have been Dixon? Did Lindop have something on Sam Dixon to force him to procure explosives, for instance? If he did, the pressure point was still there, because whatever Lindop had known, someone else knew now. Hogarth Samson.

'You asked Samson what time he got back from town, Ruby. His statement said it was about midnight. You – and Hartley – put it much earlier. But how much earlier?'

She shook her head. 'I don't know. I just saw him *leave* the site, go up to Hartley's bungalow.'

'Why did he return early anyway? *You* obviously didn't expect him back that soon.'

Ruby hesitated, looked uneasy. She was more reluctant now than she had been earlier. Perhaps she was thinking she had already talked too much. '...I don't know. Usually, when he got to drinking in town he stayed there till late. Last bus gets out here by midnight or thereabouts. That was his way. But maybe it was something to do with Chuck and him having–'

Ruby stopped suddenly. The look on her face told Crow quite plainly that she now considered she *had* said too much. He leaned forward, put his bony hand on her shoulder, gripped her hard.

'Tell me, Ruby.'

The words trickled out reluctantly. 'I ... I don't know the truth of it ... just talk, perhaps, I can't tell. It's just that ... well, when I was in the pub with Jimmie – that salesman chap – I was sitting by myself as Jimmie got some drinks and one of the gippoes came in. He saw me, knew I was Hoagy's woman. Came across, tried it on, you know, when he thought I was alone. I told him to shove off. Then Jimmie came back.'

'So?'

'Well...' Ruby wriggled uncomfortably.

222

'It's just that the gippoe started off by saying he was glad to see me alone, he'd try his luck, because it looked as though Hoagy was going to have his hands full that night. That's all.'

'No,' Crow said, watching her eyes carefully. 'There's more.'

'Honest, there isn't,' Ruby protested. 'It's just … well, we had a word, and I just got the impression that what he meant was that Hoagy was boiling up trouble for himself.'

'In another pub?'

'Yes.'

'With whom?'

'With … Chuck Lindop. They were sat in a corner, apparently, pretty intense, pretty private. Hoagy was getting mad, but Chuck was ugly. Quite ugly, if you know what I mean.'

Crow knew. 'What was the quarrel about?' he asked.

'I don't know. Really. Hoagy hasn't mentioned it – and I ain't going to ask.'

But John Crow could guess. It was something that had been puzzling him already. Witnesses had already stated that Lindop had been in Stowford that night, but there had been no apparent reason why he had returned to the site early. But if he and Samson had been together in the pub, quarrelling…

'What time do you expect Hoagy at the site tonight?' Crow asked.

2

John Crow's back was aching. The sunshine of yesterday had gone, the skies were grey and leaden, the bacon had been swimming in grease that morning, and the sandwich he had had at lunch-time had been stale. It was one of those days, and now his back was aching. He had first had trouble years ago, lifting that damned bag of cement, and now it plagued him from time to time. The physiotherapist he visited told him driving-seats of cars were bad for him, and tall men often had weak backs anyway. But a car seat sometimes gave John Crow relief; hard-backed chairs, that had not been made to accommodate either his long back or his long legs, did not.

'Any news of Samson yet?' he asked, as George Stafford came into the room and dropped some papers on his desk.

'Not a lot. He just seems to have gone to earth. We have a report here that he hired a car forty-eight hours ago and hasn't returned it. We've got a call out for the car – and for him.'

'His gipsy friends might be a possibility.'

'Yes, but they've dispersed across two counties and it'll take some checking. Still, it looks as though we've got our man.'

'Hmmm.' John Crow eased his lean buttocks on the hard chair and thought about the blessed board that normally gave him relief at home. It never bothered Martha when he put it in the bed, but then, she was the most complacent and accommodating of wives. 'You think we can present a case, then?'

'Enough to convince the magistrates.'

'Let's try it on for size.'

'Right.' Stafford stooped over the desk and riffled through the papers he had deposited there. 'First of all, by using the statements made by all the parties we've questioned, I've drawn up this timetable.'

	Lindop	Keene	Ruby Sanders	Samson	Hartley
9·30	arrives at van				
10·00		joins Lindop			
10·15	Lindop struggles with Keene at van		arrives in lane		
10·15+	dies	returns to wife			
10·20					
10·25					
10·30					sees car in lane
10·35			sees Samson in lane		
10·40			arrives at Keene van	arrives at bungalow	receives Samson
10·45					
11·00		rings for ambulance			
11·50				returns to site	

'Now using this timetable – which, incidentally, does not contain Samson's statement since his statement does not tally with

225

Hartley's and Ruby's – we can present a case to the beaks which goes roughly like this,' Stafford said. 'Lindop and Samson tried to persuade Hartley to rob Cobham Park and failed, so they went ahead with the job and bungled it. They cased Northleach Hall some time later and again Lindop tried to "persuade" Hartley, who responded fearfully by agreeing to come in with them but also by grassing anonymously to us, so we'd put a watch on the Hall.' He paused. 'We get that much from Hartley.'

'Not the most reliable of witnesses, in view of his past record, but go on.'

'The next stage is reached when Lindop begins to realize Hartley's condition is a bit dicky, and the Hall itself is coming under police surveillance.'

'We don't know he ever realized that,' Crow murmured.

'No, sir, but it's a reasonable supposition. Because our case will be that Lindop began to realize the game wasn't really on, with a lukewarm Hartley and a Hall crawling with coppers. So he wanted to pull out. We have it in the statement of Mrs Lindop, and others, that he was rough and wild – but he also knew when to call a halt.'

'But Hogarth Samson did not?'

'Exactly. The night he died, Lindop met Samson in Stowford. He told Samson he intended calling Northleach Hall off. Samson

226

remonstrated with him, they argued, things got tense. We have Ruby Sanders's evidence for that–'

'Hearsay.'

'–and once we get our hands on Samson's gipsy friend we'll be able to support it.'

'You *hope* we'll be able to support it.'

Stafford cleared his throat noisily and sniffed. 'Right. The upshot of the argument was that Lindop went back to the site in a nasty frame of mind. Keene can vouch for that – it accounts for part of Lindop's loss of temper in his fracas with Keene. Anyway, Lindop was at the site by nine-thirty, having driven back. Keene arrived at his van at ten, the generator was blown about twelve minutes after ten, there was the brief struggle between Keene and Lindop, and Keene returned to his wife. Almost *immediately*, Samson arrived.'

Stafford leaned forward, took another sheet of paper from the desk. 'Normally, there's only one bus out at that time, but the ten-twenty, the regular bus, was preceded by a relief bus – laid on for the fair. That one arrived at twelve minutes after ten – just about when the generator went up – and was followed by the regular service bus at ten-twenty. Samson couldn't have been on the ten-twenty, or Ruby would have seen him walk down the lane to the site, since she and her salesman were parked in the lane about ten-fifteen or shortly afterwards. We're still trying to get hold of the people who were on those buses, and with a bit of luck we'll get the evidence we need again – that Samson was on the ten-twelve.'

'We might also try Sam Dixon,' Crow said thoughtfully. 'If we assume he did blow the generator, he *might* have seen Samson enter the lane a couple of minutes later.'

'Right. It's now ten-fifteen. As he comes down the site Samson sees Keene returning to his van. Samson continues the quarrel with Lindop, who is still excited after the Keene struggle and takes a swing at him. Samson picks up the crowbar and bashes him, just once. He's big enough and stupid enough and dangerous enough to do it. Maybe he just stands there a moment. Maybe he doesn't realize Lindop is dying. But there's just the chance he went into the van and looked for Lindop's deposit – the money he believed that Lindop had. It wasn't there, but Samson discovered where it was. He found the number of the hotel deposit box. So, within ten minutes, about ten thirty-three, he ups and aways from there, hurries up the lane, passes Ruby in the car and goes to Hartley's bungalow. He stays there until eleven-fifty, by which time the site is crawling with people, and then he returns, innocence itself. Next morning he meets his gipsy friends, gets one of them to collect the money from the hotel and another to fix him an alibi for the night of the murder, and there it is. But we've got him because we can prove he left that site at ten thirty-five and returned just over an hour later. And that is in direct contradiction to his own statement, made the night of the murder.'

Crow nodded thoughtfully. 'It looks not bad, not bad at all. But there's still some corroborative evidence needed–'

'We're working on it.'

'And there are still a few avenues we haven't explored completely.'

'Sir?'

'First of all, we know there was someone else involved in Lindop's and Samson's schemes.'

Stafford pulled a face. 'We know he *exists* – we have Hartley's statement and Ruby Sanders's statement to vouch for that. But we don't know who he is. I don't think it matters too much; after all, if we can prove that Samson killed Lindop it doesn't matter too much if we *ever* find the identity of the other member of the group.'

'Except that he might supply evidence that puts a different complexion on things,' Crow said. 'What if it turned out to be Sam Dixon, for instance? It might be *he* who killed Lindop in that case, after blowing the generator, and after seeing first Keene and then Samson quarrel with Lindop.'

'There wouldn't have been time for that, sir.'

'Hmmm... Yes, and that's something else that bothers me. Time.' He hesitated for a moment, while the unbidden recollection fluttered at the back of his mind again, only to dance once more out of reach. He sighed. 'You know, this time thing is a problem. It's all so ... *hurried.* I mean, look at your sketched timetable. Everything of import-ance seems to have happened within a period of thirty minutes, but look at the coming and going that went on in that time! Everyone regarded the site as all but deserted, and yet there's Keene, and Ruby, and Lindop himself, and Samson – and maybe Dixon too – all buzzing about on the site. Yet only one person, really, gets observed: Samson, by Ruby. You see what I mean?'

Stafford nodded. 'I do, but they are *individual* movements. And thirty seconds, a minute or so, is enough for one person to take the stage and never see the other actor go to the wings.'

Crow smiled. 'It's getting like that, though, George. A game. An act. Villain enters left and all that.'

'It's all possible,' Stafford said, a little stiffly.

'I agree. As it's also possible that *Forsyth* might have got angry enough to kill Lindop, though we can't tie a visit to the site that evening to him.' He thrust out his pendulous lower lip and considered the matter for a moment. 'And one of the lynch-pins is Ruby Sanders. The blow that struck down our friend Lindop *could* have been wielded by Ruby. It didn't take much force to kill Lindop.'

'But she wouldn't have had time to do him in,' Stafford protested. 'She left the salesman only *after* she saw Samson go to Hartley's bungalow. And by that time it's probable that Lindop had already been struck down.'

'I take the point. Even so, I think we still need corroborative evidence,' Crow said.

'We've had a couple of men going over Samson's van. With luck we'll find something there.'

Crow grunted non-committally. 'There's still one person we haven't mentioned as a possibility.'

'Sir?'

'Andrew Keene.'

George Stafford inclined his head on one side like a wise sheepdog observing a recalcitrant ram. 'Not overlooked. But discounted, I think.'

'Tell me why?'

'Well, reading between the lines as much as anything, and chatting with people on the site, I get the general picture of Andrew Keene as pretty much a quiet character with a wife who'd *like* to wear the pants, at least. She's been dissatisfied, certainly. But when you come down to it, though he had that flare-up at work and clobbered that driver, it doesn't look as though he was *committed* in the same way when he went after Lindop. I mean, what was it all about? A receipt for the sale of the van. Sure, Sara Keene was anxious and she needled him into going to have it out with Lindop, but I think Andrew Keene had to stoke up the fires of resentment even to go there to the van. And even if he had had a couple of drinks, he wasn't stoked up enough – not enough to commit murder.'

'They had a struggle.'

'But there were no marks on Lindop, and Keene's story is he got bundled out of the van.'

'Couldn't that humiliation have been enough to stir him?' Crow asked.

'He'd have been more likely to have gone stumbling off into the darkness to be by himself, in my estimation,' Stafford replied seriously. 'Except that he had a pregnant wife back at his van – and when he got back she started into labour. No, I think Keene is telling us the truth and besides, there's a hell of a lot running against Hogarth Samson right now.'

'Maybe too much.'

'I don't mind, as long as it's enough for the beaks.'

John Crow stretched, in a vain effort to ease the ache in his back. He rose stiffly. 'All right, I'll go along with that summary for the time being. So let's get ourselves organized. You've got to continue the check on the gipsies to see if we can find Samson's friend – and maybe Samson himself – and if we can also get Samson's alibi broken *and* find the man who took out Lindop's deposit we'll really be in luck. As for me, I'm getting out for a while.'

'Where can I contact you, if I need to?'

Crow stood upright and flexed the muscles in his back. With luck, they'd ease his discs back into place and get rid of this pain. Otherwise, maybe the car seat would do it, even if the physiotherapist told him he was merely storing up trouble for himself. 'I'm taking the squad car. No driver necessary. While you continue with the gipsies and forensic I'm going up to Foxholes Quarry again. If I can persuade Sam Dixon to trust me, maybe he'll come up with something. Apart from him, there's young Keene. We had one chat and he opened up. Maybe he'll do it again.'

'What are you hoping he'll come up with?' Stafford asked.

'He might have seen Samson coming on the site. He wouldn't necessarily have told us – after all, he's not given Sam Dixon away even though he must know we'll probably be able to show it *was* Dixon who blew that generator. You might wonder why he'd protect Samson, but it's not that. I think Andrew Keene is a peculiarly *loyal* person. He doesn't know Samson killed Lindop; even if he saw Samson there that night, unless he actually had incriminating evidence against the man he wouldn't talk. But it could be enough for us to proceed. If I can get him to talk.'

'He might also have seen Sam Dixon.'

'There is that possibility. But we'll check. Right, I'll see you later.'

Stafford nodded, a little glumly. He was probably somewhat fed-up at the thought that he would be staying in the office while Crow was out and about. Crow was affected by a momentary stab of sympathy, but it was overridden by a more physical stab of pain in his back. He headed for the door.

The phone rang.

Stafford reached for it. He picked it up, listened for a moment, then turned his head towards Crow.

'It's for you.'

Crow came back, took the phone from Stafford.

'Chief Inspector Crow.'

'Ah ... this is Honey Lindop.'

'Can I help you?'

'Well ... I'm not sure. It's just that I...' There was a pause. John Crow caught Stafford's glance. The hell with it, he thought. John Crow might be in charge of this murder investigation, but George Stafford was a man better equipped to deal with women like Honey Lindop.

'Mrs Lindop – look, I'm sorry, but I'm just on the way out. Perhaps you'd like to have a chat with my colleague Inspector Stafford.'

He handed the phone over. Wordlessly, Stafford took it. He listened, then frowned, raised his eyebrows. 'She hung up,' he said plaintively. Crow's back twinged and he walked out of the office and into the Broadway. The sky wanted to pour rain down on him, but held it back sullenly.

Colonel Hodges, the quarry manager, was ex-Eton, ex-Hussars, and a whisky and cigars man who had known several of the top brass at New Scotland Yard when he had spent some time in the Ministry of Defence in the fifties. He told John Crow all about it and asked questions, some pertinent, some impertinent, about the Lindop investigation, the birch, capital punishment and didn't John Crow think the answer to it all was conscription? Crow was glad to make his escape to seek out Sam Dixon.

Not that the interview was productive. Sam Dixon was a close-mouthed Cotsaller who didn't like detectives from London and made no secret of the fact. He admitted nothing. When Crow hinted at the reasons behind his wife leaving him he said it was his own business; when Crow was more direct and suggested the breakdown of the marriage had been the result of her liaison with Chuck Lindop, Dixon just stared at him wordlessly, neither admitting nor denying the fact. And it was the same story with the dynamite.

Sam Dixon listened while Crow suggested that Dixon had nothing to fear if only he would tell the truth. He had taken the dynamite from the stores, hadn't he? He had intended getting revenge on Lindop by blowing up the generator and causing him inconvenience? If Dixon would admit it, the whole matter could be dealt with quietly and with no fuss – for John Crow had more important fish to fry.

'The important thing, Mr Dixon, is that I should know what you saw that night. That generator went up just after ten. What I want to know – *need* to know – is whether you saw anyone else in the lane about that time, either coming or going.'

Sam Dixon was unmoved. 'How could I,' he asked, 'if I wasn't even there?'

3

The minutes ticked away and John Crow sat

there, saying little, while Andrew's nervous system began to feel the strain. The early questions Crow had asked had been about Sam Dixon again, and Andrew had pattered out the same answers he had given previously: dynamite had been taken, but he had no idea by whom, and he certainly was not able to confirm that it had been Sam Dixon who took it. Crow's lugubrious face had seemed to lengthen, and the deep-set eyes had become ever unhappier, but Andrew couldn't help that. Sam Dixon was not a friend of his, but he and Sam had one thing in common: they had both been wronged by Chuck Lindop, and Andrew was not prepared to give away Sam's secret. At least Sam had had the guts to take a stand – he had stolen the dynamite, blown that generator, and for that he had to be admired. So Andrew was not the man to give him away.

'One thing puzzles me,' Crow was saying as he leaned forward, bony elbows resting on packing case still unopened. 'We've been sifting through the statements – you know, Andrew, on a case like this there are literally hundreds, if not thousands of statements we have to go through, and the idea is to pick out those items which agree or conflict one with another and which are important to the investigation. In this case, the statements we've taken, they all agree more or less on events and places and times – with one exception. But that exception causes problems. It's just that you don't mention having seen anyone on the site.'

'I don't understand,' Andrew said.

'Well, times are so crucial, of course, and it's possible that the very moment when the murderer came on the site you were already back in your van. You say in your statement that you struggled with Lindop, he threw you out and you went back to your van, where you stayed until Ruby Sanders arrived. So I suppose you could have just missed Hoagy Samson.'

'Samson?' Andrew's mouth was dry and his voice came out as a croak. 'He didn't come to the site until later, around midnight I think, when everyone was milling around.'

Crow nodded. 'That's the supposition we've been working on. Until we started checking statements. And it's led to us putting out a call for Hogarth Samson, suspicion of murder, although the official statement will be he's needed to help us in our enquiries.'

'Suspicion of *murder*?' Andrew's armpits were cold with perspiration. 'But why should you think Samson killed Lindop?'

Crow held up a bony finger and inspected it gloomily. 'They quarrelled in Stowford.' He raised a second finger. 'They were involved in criminal activity and fell out over it.' A third finger flicked out. 'He was on the site much earlier than midnight–'

'But that's not so!' Andrew hesitated, confused. 'I mean, I'd have seen him if he'd come on, surely–'

'You went back to your van,' Crow interrupted. 'But think back to your phone call to the hospital. Was there anything *unusual* in your visit to Hartley's bungalow?'

Andrew shook his head. 'I don't know what you mean.'

'When you got to the bungalow, was there anything odd in Hartley's behaviour? Did he seem nervous, tense, anything like that?'

'I can't really say…' Andrew frowned, bit his lip as he thought back to that night. It had been a confused time, a frightened time, and he could not remember too clearly. But Hartley had seemed odd… 'He didn't really want to let me in, I remember that. I mean, he didn't try to stop me, but he seemed sort of reluctant.'

'And when you were inside the bungalow?'

'Yes… When I'd finished the call, I .. well, I didn't really want to go back to the site. It's not something I can explain too well, but Sara was crying there and Ruby was looking after her and I was sort of in the way, you know what I mean? So I didn't want to go back, not straight away, and if Hartley had offered me a drink I'd have welcomed it. But he didn't. He just stood there. It was as though he wanted me to go.'

Crow's eyes were sad. 'Anything more than just wanting you to go, Andrew?'

'More?'

'Did you get the impression he was not alone?'

Andrew ran a dry tongue over dry lips. 'I … I can't be sure. He did seem nervous, and he stood against the door to the living-room as though he was barring it–'

'Yes,' Crow nodded. 'That's just what he was doing. He didn't want you to know that Lindop's murderer was in there. He was hiding him – though maybe he didn't know at that point of time that the man was a murderer.'

'You … you mean–'

'Hoagy Samson. After you left Lindop Samson killed him. Ruby saw him leave the site and go to Hartley's bungalow. Hartley has told us Samson came there. Your remarks confirm things a little more. It gives us enough – and we've got a call out for him now.' The deep-set eyes bored into Andrew, making him feel that his very thoughts were being subjected to a searching analysis. 'Is there anything you want to add, Andrew?'

'I … I can't believe that Mr Samson–'

'Why not?'

'Well … I don't know … I mean, I didn't see him on the site and I *was* the only person…' His voice died away as Crow waited. He couldn't get out the words he should have said, and his mind was full of the dark images of that terrible night when the ache still stirred in his groin and the cold iron was in his hand and Chuck Lindop was turning to look at him.

'We're pretty sure it was Samson,' Crow said quietly. 'And when we find him, we'll get the story we want.'

Crow waited a little while as though still hoping Andrew would speak but there was nothing Andrew could say. He sat there dumbly, until at last Crow rose, nodded goodbye and headed for the door. Only when the silence of the storeroom rushed in on him did Andrew start up. He almost ran to the door and stared wildly out to the road when Crow was about to get into the squad car. He wanted to call out, tell Crow he was making a mistake, but the words choked in his throat. It was something he could not do; the police wouldn't make such a mistake; Samson wouldn't be held responsible...

Crow was in the car, apparently listening to the car radio. He was sitting there, his bald head cocked on one side, like a great black bird of prey, waiting to hurtle out of the sky on its victim. Yet Andrew knew he wasn't really like that. His voice could be gentle, his eyes calm and sympathetic...

'Andrew!' Crow had replaced the microphone and was leaning out of the car, beckoning. Andrew jerked spasmodically like a puppet in the hands of an inexperienced master, and then he walked towards the car. Crow looked up at him. His eyes seemed black and snapping. 'Andrew – you know where Horse Bottom Quarry is?'

His tone was harsh and peremptory. Andrew nodded. 'Yes. It's deserted now and–'

'Get in. I want you to guide me there.'

John Crow drove swiftly and expertly. The ache that had been plaguing him was now forgotten. The suspicions that had been drifting through his mind, the doubts that had been raised by Andrew's nervousness, those were now washed away as the more imperative need for action arose.

The rounded, wooden hills were all about them in the grey afternoon; they drove through little villages and across narrow bridges under Andrew's direction, but John Crow hardly noticed the countryside. He concentrated on his driving, and on the images that flashed through his brain.

He should have stayed at the station to speak to Mrs Lindop when she phoned through. She must have heard from Samson then – been uncertain what to do. The delay in speaking to George Stafford had given her the chance to change her mind, decide on a course of action. Crow's journey to see Dixon and Andrew Keene had been a waste of time anyway; he would have been better employed questioning Honey Lindop.

'How much farther?' he asked harshly.

'About two miles,' Andrew replied.

Crow glanced at his watch. It had been closer than he realized. Filkins lay below them now as they began to climb and he guessed the squad cars wouldn't get there before him. The problem that arose now was Andrew. First chance he got, Crow would drop Andrew, keep him well away from trouble.

'What's happening?' Andrew asked.

'The end of it all, I hope,' Crow said shortly. 'Where's the quarry?'

'Just up ahead,' Andrew said. 'But who are you expecting to see up there?'

'Hogarth Samson,' Crow said grimly. 'The call I had in the car was to tell me that Samson's gipsy friend has been picked up and the word *murder* has made him burst into song.' He shot a quick glance in Andrew's direction and saw the puzzlement in his face. 'There's no time to explain now, but I want to pull in somewhere, let you out, and then when the squad cars come you can wave them down, tell them I've gone up ahead and will be waiting for them. Here – this'll do.'

He swung the car violently, braking hard, and it brushed the bushes overhanging the narrow layby under the cliff. John Crow almost pushed Andrew out.

'When they come, tell them I'm up ahead.'

He slammed the door shut, drove out of the layby and accelerated fiercely into the bend. The engine whined as the car moved into the steep slope, there was a momentary lull as though the world were suspended and then Andrew heard the sound of the crash.

4

The road was steep and narrow. It twisted up the hillside like a slow snake, flanked by bushes, alder, silver birch, and the hill itself seemed to merge with the dark, sullen sky. After the sound of the rending metal there had been silence, as though the hill was shocked by the violence of the crash, and as Andrew ran up the hill the only sound seemed to be the crunching of his feet on the old, crumbling roadway that led to the deserted quarry, and the harsh rasp of his breath against the late afternoon air.

The quarry itself was disused now. Its heyday was over, and the steep cliffs where the stone had been torn away to build the houses that made the Cotswolds famous for their beauty were stark and stiff with regrets, naked and harsh, forbidding in their severe wounds. Andrew had come up here often enough as a boy but it had been some years since he had visited it last. But he remembered how the road twisted upwards, and finally levelled out into an open area at the foot of the last hilltop. It was there that the last lorries had completed their final turning circles, laden with stone; it was there that the last huts had stood, now deserted and fallen into crumbling decay.

The cars stood some fifty yards from the broadening of the road.

Andrew's step slowed. He approached the cars, heard the slow ticking of heated metal as it cooled, heard the slow gurgle of spilled petrol. The squad car must have met the older hired car as it came out of the quarry; Crow must have tried to block the other car by swinging the police vehicle directly into its path. The manœuvre had obviously failed to intimidate the other driver; from the state of the two cars he had driven hard into Crow and the impact had crushed the bonnets of both vehicles.

Feeling slightly sick, Andrew steeled himself to look inside the cars. They were both empty. In spite of the force of the crash, both drivers would seem to have escaped. Andrew looked around him; he could see no one, near no one. He walked forward quickly towards the quarry itself.

In the fading light the quarry was an eerie, stark place of dark shadows, broken stone, the littered debris of a dead industry. Scattered bushes fringed the cliff-like edge of the drop; the fence was broken in places, the iron stanchions that barred the edge to the public were rusted and leaning at crazy angles.

'Inspector Crow!' Andrew shouted, and the quarry picked up the sound, converted it into a rumble of discontent at being disturbed from its twenty-year sleep, and sent echoes growling down into the raw places where stone had been ripped away by chisel and saw and dynamite.

Andrew tried again, and moved across the empty clearing towards the last of the tumbledown huts, and then he stopped, rooted to the spot as the echoes died away, lingering regretfully in the darkness that crept up over the quarry.

The woman was lying on her face, one arm crumpled under her. She was wearing a dark windcheater and blue slacks that were tight across her body. He had the feeling he had seen her before but he could not be sure; certainly, her hair – the colour of tin – was familiar, though when he had last seen her it had not been matted with the slow seep of blood. He knelt on the ground beside her, put out a tentative hand and touched her shoulder as though fearful that she might not really be there, but was rather a figment of his imagination. She was real.

He slipped his hand inside the front of her windcheater, under her blouse, and her flesh was still warm. But suddenly she was changing, and it wasn't a woman he saw there but a man, and he recoiled as the picture of the woman lying in front of him became blurred with another mental image, the image of Lindop, who had died from a blow to the head.

The rattling of stones brought Andrew back to the present with a start. He looked wildly around him in the gathering darkness, intensely conscious of the injured woman at his feet and the presence somewhere in the quarry of the man who had attacked her.

But where was Inspector Crow?

A boulder crashed on the quarry face, skittered away into the echoing darkness. Andrew turned and picked his way past the rusted stanchions, under the broken wire and moved to the edge of the quarry. It was a great black hole in the ground; above his head the bruised, darkening sky made it almost impossible to see anything in the quarry, but he could hear the scrambling, panting sound interspersed with running, rattling, bouncing rocks. There was some-one in the quarry, making his way up over the lip, painfully and with difficulty.

Andrew stood still, his heart hammering against his ribs. He was a child again, con-fronting the unknown on the bend of the stairs and the hairs on the back of his neck prickled. A few moments later he saw the movement on the lip of the quarry.

'Inspector Crow?'

A sound came, a wheezing, grunting sound. Andrew stepped forward gingerly. The crumbling, rain-rotted rock at the edge of the quarry was unsafe; years of exposure to the wind and rain after a period when the tools had dug and split and hacked away at its face had left it perched, ready to fall under pressure, collapse under the weight of a man's foot.

'Andrew...'

The head seemed almost white in the darkness except for the dark stain across the brow where the blood ran. It was a death's head rising out of the darkness of the quarry, a staring face, mouth open with effort, gasping, a bony hand grasping at tufts of tough grass, pulling upwards, painfully, inch by inch.

'Andrew...'

The fingers were lean and hard and powerful. Lying on his stomach with legs braced apart and arm extended Andrew felt the bony fingers grasp at his wrist, take fierce purchase, drag at him until he thought his arm was going to be pulled out of his socket. He wriggled backwards as the second hand took hold of his elbow and he could see Crow's glaring features, twisted with effort, just below him. He strained, pulling, and there was a lurch as Crow found a foothold, took some of his own weight and lifted himself up over the crumbling edge of the quarry.

He lay there for several minutes, panting hoarsely. Andrew sat beside him, saying nothing. At last Crow raised his head, looked across to the roadway where the woman lay.

'She alive?'

Andrew nodded. Painfully, Crow got up to a sitting position. 'How can we get down into the quarry itself? Is there a pathway?'

'The far side. But it's dangerous.'

Crow nodded. They sat there silently for a moment, just six feet from the edge of the drop, but somehow the thought of moving back seemed not to occur to them. The danger in which Crow had found himself was now over, and he simply sat there thoughtfully, staunching the blood flowing from his cut brow with a handkerchief as though this were all a mundane affair. The shudders that occasionally racked Andrew's body brought home to them both the realities of their surroundings, however, and as the first squad car came up the hill, headlights glancing whitely across the quarry, Crow rose to his feet, helped Andrew to rise. They walked across to the woman and Crow removed his jacket, placed it gently over her. Her eyelids were fluttering. He knelt beside her, holding her shoulders.

All at once the quarry seemed to be full of people. Police officers got out of the three cars, Andrew recognized Inspector Stafford and one or two constables he had seen from time to time in Stowford. He stood to one side, waiting, as they spoke to Crow, and after a while a group of policemen made their way across to the far side of the quarry and began the scramble down the pathway to the bottom. Their flashlights danced and lifted against the crumbling rock; they disappeared from view and then there was only the fading glow arising from the depths.

An ambulance came klaxoning its way up the hill, and the blue lights flashing around the clearing added a macabre touch to the scene. Inspector Crow walked across to Andrew.

'I'm going back now, to get this attended to,' he touched his bloodied brow. 'You'd better come as well. You don't look too good.' He spoke softly, a father to a son, quiet, sympathetic. Andrew nodded and together they went to the police car. Only when they were seated inside did Andrew look across to Chief Inspector Crow.

'Who's down there?' he asked.

The squad car lurched and turned, bearing them away from the site. Crow's sad eyes stared at Andrew, and then were hooded.

'Hogarth Samson,' he said in a tired, defeated voice.

5

Everything was so bright. The walls were painted a bright, pale green. The flowers were bright red; the curtains shone, the sheets on the bed were dazzling and as the sun poured a golden light through the window even the nurse on the ward seemed to sparkle.

Sara looked beautiful.

'I don't really know why I still need to stay in bed,' she said. 'I mean, it's been days, and I feel fine now.'

Andrew squeezed her hand. She didn't *look* fine; she was beautiful but it was a new kind of beauty for her. There was a transparency about her skin that had never been there before, a delicacy about her complexion that was new. Her eyes had changed; he had seen panic in them often enough in the old days but since the baby had arrived it was as though she had acquired a new wisdom, a new realization of life that transformed her. And the way she held his hand denoted, to him, a new dependence – not the greedy, demanding dependence he had resisted before for its selfishness, but a dependence based upon trust.

'You're looking well, anyway,' he said. 'And I've got some news that'll perk you up further. I applied for a job at the week-end, in Oxford. Had a letter this morning. I think I stand a chance of getting it. Ten quid a week more than I'm getting. Maybe we'll be able to get a house.'

'Oh, Andrew,' she said and squeezed his hand. There was the glint of tears in her eyes. 'I'm sorry about–'

'Hush,' he interrupted her, rather more sharply than he had intended. There was an awkward silence for a moment. To break it, he said, 'They'll be bringing the baby back in soon, won't they?'

'It's near feeding time,' she said. Her eyes searched his face, anxiety flickering deep in her glance. 'Her breathing is fine now and she's putting on weight. Are you going to wait?'

He did not meet her glance but looked away down the ward. There were a number of men there, sitting with their wives, a couple of grandmothers and relatives, most seemed happy and bright. And in the far doorway was a figure he recognized. His stomach lifted and dropped. He half rose from his seat as the tall bony figure moved into the ward. Detective Chief Inspector Crow looked around, caught sight of Andrew, and came forward. He had a piece of sticking plaster above his left eye, otherwise he seemed none the worse for the encounter at Horse Bottom Quarry two nights previously. He nodded to Andrew and smiled at Andrew's wife. He stood beside the bed.

'Hello, Mrs Keene. This is the first time we've met. I'm John Crow.'

Sara sat stiffly in bed, her face frozen into a nervous mask, her mouth slightly open. Crow put out his hand and after a moment she shook hands with him.

'Do you mind if I sit down for a moment?' he asked. 'I just came in for a few minutes, to pay my respects to Mrs Keene, and to offer a more ... formal thank you to Andrew, for the way he helped me the other evening. I didn't really explain what had happened.'

'There was something about it in the papers,' Sara managed.

'Ah, well, not the full story... What actually happened was that after I dropped Andrew I drove up the hill and met Samson driving out. I tried to block him, he crashed into me, scrambled out and ran back towards the quarry.' Crow smiled ruefully and touched the sticking plaster on his forehead. 'It's axiomatic that detective chief inspectors of a somewhat advanced age do not go running after younger criminals, on the assumption that youth is more likely to get the upper hand. And chief inspectors are not exactly ten a penny. But ... well, rather foolishly, I gave chase. And since my legs are longer than his and over about fifty yards I can manage a reasonable sprint – though after that I'm done – I caught him by the shoulder and spun him around. It was then that he hit me. I hung on, we staggered through the fence, and before I knew where I was I was hanging grimly on to his leg at the edge of the quarry. He overbalanced, we both went over the edge. I let go...' His sad eyes lingered over Andrew. 'I was pretty near the end of my tether when you came along. I couldn't really see too well. I'm grateful for your help.'

'Samson fell to his death,' Andrew muttered uncomfortably.

'Broken neck,' Crow said. His eyes were clouded. 'I didn't want things to happen that way... Still, I shouldn't talk about the case when I come visiting a beautiful woman who has just produced a daughter–'

'Have ... have you closed the case then?' Sara asked in a subdued, hesitant tone.

Crow stared at her thoughtfully, and then nodded. 'The local police, Inspector Stafford and the rest, they're all agreed it's over. It ended with Samson's death.'

'The woman at the quarry–'

'That was Honey Lindop, Chuck Lindop's widow. I thought she was dead when I got there, but apart from a nasty blow on the head she'll be all right now.'

'But what was she doing there?'

Crow took a deep breath. 'Well, it was like

254

this. Chuck Lindop was a small-time crook, but he could fascinate women. And Honey was still ... wanting him, I suppose. Even after they separated she was still on reasonable terms with him, and after she started working for the estate agents Chuck came to her with a proposition. If she could feed him inside information, he could carry out some burglaries and they'd split the proceeds. I think she went along with it in the first instance in the hope it would somehow weld them back again – later, I imagine she just enjoyed the extra money. Not that there was much of it. As far as I can gather Chuck didn't even play fair on the split.'

'She's told you this?'

Crow nodded. 'And a little more. She undertook a valuation at Cobham Park and gave Chuck the layout of the place. She took no other direct part in it, but Fred Hartley wouldn't get involved so it was bungled by Lindop and Samson. They needed a pro like Hartley. Later, when Honey gave Lindop information on Northleach Hall Lindop tried to force Hartley in – but he adopted his own way of wriggling out of it successfully. Lindop called off the job.'

Crow glanced at Andrew, who failed to look at him.

'Since both Samson and Lindop are now dead,' Crow continued, 'some of the rest must be guesswork. But it seems as though

Lindop and Samson quarrelled. Samson wanted to continue, Lindop wanted to call Northleach off. The upshot of it all was that in a rage Samson came back to the site, continued the quarrel, killed Lindop, hid for a while at Hartley's and then put the pressure on him again. He recruited his gipsy friend Billy to collect the money from Lindop's hotel deposit box and just beat Honey to it. She was mad as hell.'

'How ... how much of this can be proved?' Andrew asked huskily. 'The ... the murder, I mean.'

'We've got statements that fix timings. We've got a speck of blood on a shoe of Samson's that proves at the very least that he stood near Lindop's corpse, even if we can't prove he killed him. It's all very circumstantial–'

'But you said–' Sara bit back the words as Crow stared at her. After a moment, he continued.

'Circumstantial, but it fits. Anyway, we were running around in circles and for a few days Samson felt safe. The money from the hotel wasn't as much as he'd expected, and he was obsessed with Northleach Hall, but when he heard we had pulled Hartley in for questioning he decided we were getting too close. He went to earth. He hired a car, drove to his gipsy friends and brooded.'

'You can't mean he still wanted to break

into Northleach?'

'I told you. It was an obsession. He'd killed Lindop over it. He was angry at Hartley's refusal. But he could still do it *alone,* and cock a snook at us all. Better, he could do it *and others,* if he got the same sort of assistance Chuck had.' Crow smiled sadly. 'I think you have to remember how Samson was. He had followed Lindop in everything. In this way, maybe, he'd be going one better. And that was important.' He hesitated, then went on. 'When I was with Andrew at Foxholes I had a call from headquarters. They'd pulled in the gipsy Billy, and mention of the word murder had started him talking fit to bust. He told us that Samson had phoned Honey Lindop, arranged to meet her. Now she had already called in to speak to me – I'd handed her over to my colleague and she dried up. I think she changed her mind. At that point she intended coming clean, but when she couldn't speak to me she changed her mind, decided to go through with it and meet Samson. She thought she could handle him; threaten him perhaps, get back some of Lindop's money, because she was still furious that Samson had got there first. All we knew when I got that call at Andrew's quarry at Foxholes was that they were meeting at Horse Bottom Quarry, of course, but Honey has filled in the rest. The fact was, she *couldn't* handle him. He wanted to start the whole thing going again, get her to feed information to him – he even suggested they shack up together, she tells me. And all *she* wanted was a share of the money he'd lifted from that deposit box. As you might imagine, they didn't see eye to eye. And her contempt for him, her threats, got him into a blind rage.'

Crow frowned, and shook his head.

'I don't think he intended trying to kill her. But he could see all his ideas going up in smoke, he felt cornered, and he just didn't really know what to do. His intellect is not of the greatest. He felt trapped, I think, and his reaction was to beat his way out of it. She tells me she screamed when they quarrelled, he hit her, she fell, and then he kicked her a glancing blow on the head. After that, as far as I can make out, he just wanted to get away from there. And I arrived. I was lucky. His head hit the windscreen in that smash, and he went staggering away, half dazed. Otherwise, I could have been the one at the bottom of the quarry.'

Andrew licked his lips. 'Did … did Mrs Lindop say that Samson admitted killing her husband?'

'No. They didn't talk about it. He just wanted her to have the arrangement with him that she'd had with Lindop. He didn't admit it to the gipsy, either, but we think we've got a case circumstantially: Lindop's blood on Samson's shoe, his diary – detailing the hotel deposit box – in Samson's pocket; the timing of events the night Lindop died. And yet...' He stopped speaking, looked at the young couple and smiled gently. 'It's a funny thing, being involved in so much crime. My wife, she says I'm like an old woman, with the *feeling* I get about things. And I've got an odd feeling about this. But maybe she's right. I *am* getting to be an old woman.'

Neither Andrew nor Sara spoke. Crow hesitated, began to rise, then looked behind him as he saw Andrew's face stiffen. A nurse was advancing down the ward with a bundle in her arms. Crow smiled. 'Talking of old women, and here we have a young one.'

The nurse smiled at the three of them and put the baby in the cot beside the bed. She told Sara she would be back with the bottle in just a few minutes and then she walked away again, out of the ward. John Crow watched her go, then turned to the cot. He leaned over it and looked at the baby.

'She's a fine child,' he said after a moment.

Andrew was staring at him blankly. Sara sat rigidly in the bed, seemingly unable to move. She made no attempt to touch the child. Crow watched the little girl as she screwed up her face, knuckled a tiny fist against her cheek.

'She's doing well for a premature baby,'

Crow said quietly.

Sara found her voice. 'I ... I should be able to take ... take her home in a week or so.'

The silence grew around them as Crow continued to watch the baby's small movements. But he was no longer seeing the child, he was listening to the words people had said, watching the images cross his mind, selecting, discarding, checking. A minute ticked past and the three were silent. At last Crow turned his head to look at Andrew.

'It's an odd thing how remarks spark off a train of thought,' he said. 'The nurse, she'll bring the bottle in a few minutes. That's what it was all about the night Lindop died – a matter of minutes. It's been fluttering away at the back of my mind for some time.'

Andrew moistened his lips, but said nothing.

'The timing always bothered me,' Crow said. 'You went to Lindop's van at ten; you left at ten-fifteen. Ruby and her salesman arrived at about the same time, say ten-seventeen, and then she joined you at your van after she saw Samson hurry up the lane at about ten thirty-five.'

'Yes.' The word came out as a whisper. Crow stared at Andrew dispassionately.

'We've assumed Hogarth Samson arrived at the site, almost literally, a minute before Ruby did, having walked from the bus-stop and the ten-twelve bus from Stowford. But what if he had come off the later bus?'

'The ten-twenty?' Andrew frowned. 'I don't see–'

'If he had, Ruby would have seen him going *down* the lane to the site, so we've assumed he *must* have come off the earlier bus, and arrived at Lindop's van as you left. But all that proceeds on the assumption that Ruby was correct in her statement.'

'I still don't understand–'

'It's been buzzing around in the back of my mind,' Crow said softly. 'Something the salesman, Glanville said. When he and Ruby arrived in the lane he switched on the radio, almost *immediately,* to get some soft romantic music to put her in the mood. They had looked at his watch and he'd told her it was ten-fifteen – but that watch was unreliable that night. The point is, they arrived, Glanville switched on the radio, and almost at once he switched it off again – because it wasn't soft music he was getting, it was a report of a fracas in Chester Street between some gipsies. It wasn't a regular broadcast, it was a local ham breaking into the frequency. But you see, it changes the whole situation. That broadcast went out at *ten twenty-eight.*'

Andrew's face was pale and the muscle in his cheek jumped involuntarily. Crow watched him carefully, and the words other people had used came clicking around in his

261

head … a dreamy person, a loyal person, he hadn't given Sam Dixon away even though he owed him nothing. In spite of that one piece of violence at his work, Andrew would have run away from Lindop that night, in utter humiliation, or so Inspector Stafford suggested. A *loyal* person, a man who almost a year ago had become moody and depressed and had taken a piece of chain to a driver called Baker… But what had Mrs Lindop said when they were looking for the motive behind the generator explosion? '…married to someone working at the quarry…'

'I can't see that a few minutes make that much difference,' Andrew said.

'No?' Crow stared at him, not seeing him; instead, there was the darkness, and a man running across a field, another lying on the ground…

'Just a minute here or there–'

'But that's what it's all about, Andrew. Minutes … half-minutes even! You going back to your van at ten-fifteen, Samson arriving by ten-twenty as Ruby entered the lane in the car behind him, Samson killing Lindop and returning to the lane at ten thirty-five! Don't you see? According to Glanville's remark about that radio programme, the *inference* must be that his watch had stopped, he and Ruby didn't get to the lane until shortly before that broadcast – say three minutes before, at ten twenty-five.

Now we've not found witnesses to say that Samson was on either the first bus or the second, but if my supposition is correct, Samson *could* have come on the second bus, arriving at ten-twenty. It doesn't make that much difference, I agree, a matter of minutes. But it does make it that much more difficult for him to have killed Lindop in the time available!'

'There ... there was ten minutes,' Andrew muttered.

'Ten minutes.' Crow nodded. 'It *could* have happened. Samson could have arrived at ten twenty-five, continued his quarrel with Lindop, murdered him, searched the van and found the diary he wanted, turned out the light and walked back through the lane by ten thirty-five. But it was easier to believe when we were working on the assumption he arrived at ten-fifteen... But, as you say, it's only minutes...'

Andrew's hands began to shake. He linked his fingers in an attempt to control them. He dared not look towards Sara.

'What ... what do you conclude from this?' he asked.

'Conclude?' Crow's brow was furrowed; he frowned as though the thoughts inside his head were painful to him. He glanced aside to the baby girl lying in the cot, the child that had arrived prematurely the day after Lindop died, and he looked at the mother, white-faced and tense in the bed. 'Any conclusions I reach are irrelevant to the enquiry now. It all raises suppositions, opens up other lines of enquiry. You see, if Samson didn't have *time* to kill Lindop – and forensic say he died about ten twenty-five – we have to ask, who the hell did? Who else had opportunity, who else had motive? Are these questions I should now ask, when Samson is dead and Lindop is dead and everything seems to be sewn up? Or shouldn't I just close the whole unhappy chapter?'

Andrew's face was anguished; there was panic in his eyes. And Sara too; her face was white and her breathing was quick. John Crow looked at them both, and at the baby in the cot. Slowly, he reached his decision.

'It's all about justice, really, isn't it? The wicked shall be punished. But where does the wickedness start, and where does the punishment end? And justice... Look at Sam Dixon and Jack Forsyth – it would seem Dixon won't be brought to task over the generator, because Forsyth is going to close the site anyway and isn't interested in chasing the matter up. Is that justice for Forsyth? He's lost money over the whole thing – Sam Dixon's lost a wife. How does *he* feel? And what about Honey Lindop – all right, she was weak, and worked on the criminal fringes in a petty way, but all she really wanted was Lindop. For that matter, were Chuck Lindop's crimes so heinous?'

He turned his sad eyes on Andrew.

'And if Samson didn't kill Lindop, who did? If Lindop was already dead, and Samson found him there, then searched him for the diary and made off, where was the real killer? Who else was on the site? *You,* Andrew. But you told me you did not kill Lindop.' Crow shook his head slowly. 'And I *believed* you.'

He turned away and leaned over the cot, smiled at the baby.

'So we have to compromise,' he said softly. '*All* of us. We can't have complete justice; we can only, ever, have an approximation of it. The philosophers say that justice – complete justice – is the practice of entire virtue towards one's neighbours. But in life we have to settle for less than that – not entire virtue, just a part of it.'

He raised his head and looked at Sara. 'Chuck Lindop is dead, but there are all kinds of death and people can be reborn, just as relationships can be reborn out of destruction of something else. And as for Chuck Lindop and the rest of it … well, we'd be satisfied with what we have – a part of virtue.'

He straightened. His smile was a little stiff at the edges as he nodded to Sara, still white-faced in the bed. Then he turned to Andrew Keene.

'I'll wish you both luck,' he said quietly. 'But be careful how you go, Andrew.' He hesitated, looking squarely at the young man. 'And watch out ... watch out for the little one.'

When he had gone Andrew and Sara sat dumbly for several minutes. Suddenly, as though by delayed reaction, Sara began to shake. Andrew leaned over quickly, gripped her hands between his own. Her eyes were wide and staring and scared. He squeezed her hands but there was no response; her dependence was absolute and he felt strong enough to support her in a way he had never been able to do before. Some of the feeling must have been communicated to her for her eyes flickered a quick glance at him, the shaking began to subside. He was in control at last; perhaps he had been for some time. But now, he *knew* he could cope.

'Andrew–'

'Hush, Sara, don't worry–'

'Andrew, he *knows!*'

'No. No, he doesn't know. He guesses, maybe, but he doesn't know for sure. And it makes no difference.'

Her voice was low and fierce in its terror. 'But if he guesses, he'll find out, he'll do something about it, he'll–'

'No. Nothing is going to happen. He as good as told us that…'

'Oh, Andrew, I'm *scared*…'

So was Andrew. Not by John Crow's visit, for he had expected it for so long that now it was over it was a relief. John Crow couldn't *know* what had happened that night. He could appreciate the motivation, for it lay here in the ward, part of the motivating that could drive a person to murder in a flash of wild, unreasoning rage. But Crow might guess at what had really happened. He could picture how Andrew might have picked up that crowbar but let it drop again, to run away in desperate pain and humiliation to hide his disgust with himself in the darkness, less than a man. He would be able to understand how Chuck Lindop had shouted after him in derision, obscene, taunting words, and he would be able to imagine how Sara, standing at the back of Lindop's van in the darkness, listening to and watching her husband's humiliation, had stepped forward to pick up the crowbar Andrew had dropped.

It had been just one blow, but it had been struck with all the fury arising from Andrew's humiliation – and her own. For it had all lain unsaid between Sara and Andrew; it had crumbled their marriage; she had been foolish and stupid and vain; she had fallen from grace and was suffering the consequences. She had all but destroyed her marriage and it was all there in the obscenities Lindop hurled at Andrew's retreating back.

She brought the crowbar down once. The terror and the anger and the surge of horror at what she had done sent her stumbling back to the van, where the pains had started, brought on by the shock – violent, stabbing, *early* pains. She was there in her pain when Andrew returned.

Crow would have guessed as Andrew had – even though Sara had never told him, not even now. It lay between them, an unspoken, secret knowledge. Like the other unspoken knowledge, in the cot.

And John Crow understood that too. He had seen it in Andrew's eyes, and he had given Andrew his future, placed it in his hands. 'Watch out for the little one,' he had said, for he *knew.*

Andrew released Sara's hand and leaned over the cot. He hesitated, looking at the child that lay there, and suddenly the old, struggling, worm-like agonies were no longer twisting in his stomach and his heart. She was there, his condition for compromise, his part of virtue, and tentatively, with fingers that trembled slightly, he touched the baby caressingly on her soft cheek. It was the first time he had touched her.

She will be a beautiful child, he thought.

She will be a lovely girl, and when she grows up she will be as lovely as her mother – and more so. For she would have her father's wild, red-flaring hair.